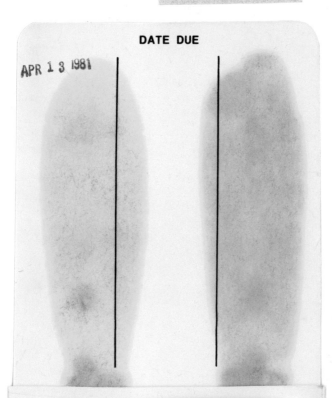

DATE DUE

APR 1 3 1981

J WEB   8/19/80

WEBER, LENORA M.   FM
    COMEBACK, WHEREVER
YOU ARE.   8. 95

HARRIS COUNTY LIBRARY
HOUSTON, TEXAS

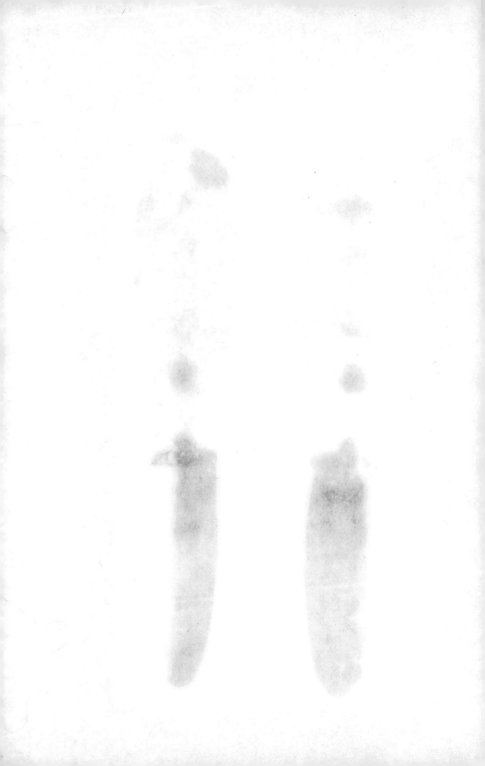

COME BACK,
WHEREVER
YOU ARE

COME BACK, WHEREVER YOU ARE

A Beany Malone Story

By Lenora Mattingly Weber

THOMAS Y. CROWELL COMPANY, NEW YORK

Published in Canada by Fitzhenry & Whiteside Limited, Toronto

Manufactured in the United States of America

L.C. Card 69-13643

ISBN 0-690-20123-0

3 4 5 6 7 8 9 10

To Harry and Jeanne

❦ I ❧

Beany Buell wakened to the thrumming of a spring rain on the roof. It was not quite dawn, and she lay in drowsy content, taking inventory of her world.

The bulk and warmth and the deep, even breathing beside her were her husband Carlton. She reached a hand out toward the window sill close to the bed. The rain was not driving in; that meant she need do nothing about the open window in the next bedroom where the two small Buells were sleeping. A dog's tongue licked her wrist as she drew her hand back; that meant that Thumper, who was sometimes absent when it came to closing up for the night, was also in under their roof.

All was right with the Buell world this chill, rainy dawn in late April.

And then she heard the sound that every mother's ear is attuned to. She might have known it was more than the pounding rain that had dragged her out of her sound sleep. Mary Elizabeth, the toddler, was rattling her crib in the next room and clamoring for attention. Thumper had come to tell her.

With wifely instinct Beany eased gently out of bed so as not to disturb her husband. He had been working on the brief of what he called a sticky case when she fell asleep, sitting up in bed, reading. She hadn't even wakened when he leveled her pillow, turned out the light, and climbed in beside her.

She groped her way out of what the real estate salesman had proudly termed the master bedroom when he showed them this low-roofed ranch house. A few steps took her into the smaller room with its two cribs, two chests of drawers, two small chairs, and two wooden buckets overflowing with toys.

In the grayish light of near dawn, Mary Elizabeth was standing up in her crib, proclaiming insistently, "Cold. Cold, Mommie—cold."

"Sh-h-h, Mary Liz, don't wake Mister."

Mister did not refer to the sleeping head of the house in the master bedroom, but to Mary Liz's slightly older brother in the next crib. Beany pushed on the night light. Mary Liz blinked delightedly. She had been named after Beany's two sisters, Mary Fred and Elizabeth, and she was like them—and unlike her mother—in that she could open her eyes and be instantly wide-awake and ready to go.

She said now quite unnecessarily, "Wet, Mommie—wet."

Oh, dear, she would have to be changed from the skin out. So would her bed. And oh, dear, again, the washing Beany had hung out yesterday was still on the line, sodden and dripping in the rain. For yesterday had been *one of those days*. Her brother Johnny, his wife, and very young daughter had left for Texas and Johnny's new job in a TV station there.

Beany had helped Miggs and Johnny close up their farmhouse on the small acreage at the edge of town, and then hurried home to cook an early supper so they could get a start on the long drive between Denver and Dallas before nightfall. That's why she hadn't brought in the washing, and why she had fallen asleep over her book without "potting" Mary Liz about eleven as usual.

That was also why Beany was so scantily covered that she was goosefleshy in the draft from the open window. Her only two nightgowns had gone through the washer, too. Now she was wearing an old shirt of her husband's, which she often did in just such an emergency and which had earned her the special and private nickname of Cutty Sark. It did not refer to the ship by that name or to the brand of Scotch whisky, but to the literal meaning of the word in Scottish—"short shirt."

Beany fumbled through the two top drawers of the bureau and found a diaper and tattered shirt. Mary Liz's wardrobe was mostly hand-me-downs from Mister. There were no nighties except the ones depending on drawstrings at the neck to hold them in place, and the drawstrings were gone. One of them would never stay on the squirmer in Beany's arms.

In the bottom drawer, and still in its tissue-paper wrapping, was a brand-new, pale-pink, fleecy robe that had been sent to Mary Liz for Christmas. Beany had been saving it for some special occasion. But here was

Mary Liz shivering and saying, "Cold—cold." Beany shook it out of its folds, untied the ribbon bow at the neck, and enveloped Mary Liz in it. The card stuck in the pocket read, "To the new little Miss Buell. Love always, Kay." *Love always to you, too, Kay.*

The fragrant scent that was part of Kay seemed to bring her gentle presence into the chilly room. It went with Beany into the kitchen where, with the baby under her left arm, she reached for an arrowroot cooky and gave it to her. Kay's hair, the color of old gold; Kay's blue eyes, sometimes laughing, often shadowed. Beany and Kay, the inseparables at Harkness High, until Kay had left for Utah with her mother. "But I'll be back, Beany," she had promised.

She *had* come back. Beany could still see that dusty Utah car stopping in front of her old home on Barberry Street, and an enraptured Kay tumbling out of it, along with a handsome giant of a husband named Joe Collins. "He's going to enroll at the U here. He's always wanted to be a phys. ed. teacher and coach. And I'm going to get a job." Kay's confident laugh had spilled over. "So Joe will come out with a B.A., and I'll have a Ph.T—meaning Putting Husband Through."

But it hadn't worked out that way. A pregnant Kay had fainted on her job. Anemia. Joe had to drop out of school and take a truck-driving job. Then when the baby had been a bouncy armful, the Joe Collinses had moved back to Peachtree, Utah. "But we'll be back," Kay had again assured Beany. "Joe and I are

4

going to save money like crazy. This working in the freezer plant for his Uncle Joe is fine for now, but you know Joe's dream of teaching phys. ed. and coaching."

What had happened to Kay's and Joe's rosy plans? Had they settled for life in Peachtree? Both Beany and Kay were desultory correspondents. But Kay herself had written once, "Don't apologize for not writing, Beany. You always know I'm *here,* and I always know you're *there."*

Beany carried Mary Liz and cooky down the hall past the room with her wet crib. Kay seemed to be still walking beside her as she had so often through Harkness's halls or later, when Kay was Mrs. Collins, through supermarket aisles where Beany would remind her, "Chicken is cheaper than steak." It was as though Kay spoke out of her troubled thoughts, "It will help just to talk things over with you, Beany."

Beany deposited Mary Liz and herself in the king-size bed with Carlton. He stirred, reached out to her, and encountered the small lump between them.

"Carl, Kay is coming back."

"Back where?"

"Back here. Back into my life."

"How do you know? Did you hear from her?"

"No, but I know anyway. It just came to me."

She waited for him to say as he always did, "You can't know anything without some basis of fact." And she was ready to answer back as she always did, with what he called a woman's illogic, "Just you wait and see."

But he was evidently not awake enough to argue. He said only, "Go to sleep." She went to sleep thinking of Kay.

It was daylight when she wakened to see a fully-clothed Carlton beside the bed. His shoulders, under a sports jacket of light-gray, nubbly tweed, looked even broader. His blond hair, still damp from the shower and showing comb marks, looked darker. His eyes were a deep blue, and usually thoughtful.

Mister was with him, also clothed. It was his pride that he could dress himself. His father nudged him, "Go on—ask her."

Thus prompted, Beany's son asked, "Would Madame like her coffee in bed?"

Mary Liz popped up like a jack-in-the-box. "Yes. Yes."

Beany pulled herself up in bed, and ran her fingers through her short, touseled hair that was several shades lighter than her eyebrows and thick lashes. A handful of freckles was spattered across her sleep-flushed face.

She said on a yawn, "Look at you two, up and dressed. And look at your lazy mother. I meant to get up early— Goodness, the sun isn't very bright—" She repeated with the aimless garrulity of someone not fully awake, "I meant to get up real early, and bring in the clothes the kids will need, and dry them by the heat—"

Carlton bent over and kissed her. "We have the

first case on the docket this morning. What were you trying to wake me up to tell me last night?"

She sat up straighter and blinked her heavy eyes. "It was early this morning. I told you Kay is coming back."

"Did she let you know she was?"

"No. But I put the robe that Kay sent her on Mary Liz, and all at once it was as though she were there with me. She was troubled about something. And she said— No, not exactly said *the words,* but I could tell she was glad she was coming because she wanted to talk something over with me."

"You married me under false pretenses, woman. You never told me you kept a crystal ball hidden in the closet." He shook his head wonderingly. "You're too much for me. Here's a copy of the night letter Western Union phoned out this morning at seven."

She took the paper, torn from the note pad beside the telephone. On it he had copied the message:

ON OUR WAY TO DENVER. CAN HARDLY WAIT TO SEE YOU.   KAY, JOE, AND JODEY COLLINS

Beany murmured, "Kay said they decided to call him Jodey because they didn't want to have big Joe and little Joe."

Her husband was still looking at her, both bewildered and amazed. "They burned witches in Salem."

"It isn't witchcraft," she said earnestly. "It's the pattern of my life. Remember, I told you once about an old woman telling me that every time a door closed in my life another would open? She meant that every time there was a lonely gap or void, it would be filled. And it's true. I've never had but two real friends. Miggs and Kay. Miggs and I were little girls together, and then she moved away, but Kay came along and filled her place. When Kay moved back to Utah, Miggs came back. And she married Johnny, so that she's a sister-in-law and best friend at the same time. Either Miggs or Kay have always been in my life."

"Birdie hop out, and crow hop in," Carl quoted an old square-dance call.

"That's right. And so yesterday Johnny and Miggs took off for Dallas, and I felt so lost—and empty. It has nothing to do with husband-wife love," she hastened to say. "And then all at once last night I could feel the door opening—"

"You must have felt the draft, Cutty Sark," he said and chuckled.

The small Mister imparted, "We made toast."

"Toast," chanted Mary Liz.

"Oh, no, little Missy, and oh, no, big Missy, not till you get up," Carlton said. "I have a hard enough life without crumbs in my bed."

Beany's giggle was cut short by Thumper's bark and the simultaneous sound of a car crunching the gravel in their driveway. She twisted herself around in bed and peered out the window. "Good grief, Uncle Matthew already. Carl, keep him from coming in. Don't let him see that I didn't get up and get your breakfast and send you off with a cheery good morning. He'll dust off his oration about a wife's duty to her husband—"

"I'll head him off." Carlton picked up his brief case.

"He's a lonely old codger," said Mister.

His parents exchanged a swift look and rueful chuckle that said, "What big ears some little pitchers have!"

Uncle Matthew Buell's stopping here at the Carlton Buell ranch house every morning had come to be a ritual. His home was farther south in one of the new, luxurious, high-rise apartment houses with maid and room service. Carlton worked with him in his law office, and over a year ago, Uncle Matthew had said, "No use taking two cars downtown, Carl, when I have to come right by your place. You leave your car for Beany, and go down in mine. I'd like you to drive. This morning and evening rush-hour traffic is getting too much for me."

So the pompous and oratorical Uncle Matthew accepted the coffee Beany poured for him each morning and took a vicarious—and often to Beany, meddlesome—interest in their lives.

He *was* a lonely old codger. He had two daughters. The married one had lived in Denver until her husband was transferred to Ohio. The unmarried artistic one preferred life in Mexico to life in Colorado. Ironically enough, while Uncle Matthew's favorite oration was on a woman's duty to home and family, his own wife spent as much time visiting her daughters as she did at home with her husband.

A car door slammed, and Beany cried out urgently, "Hurry, Carl. He's getting out to come in."

9

"I'm off, you soothsayer."

From her vantage point on her knees in the bed, and peering through an opening in the varicolored striped draperies, Beany saw the tall, impressive old gentleman hesitate as to whether he should cut across the wet lawn or follow the graveled driveway.

She saw Carlton greet him and evidently remind him they had no time to spare because of that early appearance in court. He took the driver's seat, and Uncle Matthew walked around the car and reluctantly got in on the other side.

Beany watched the car back out of the driveway and start down their street which was euphemistically named Laurel Lane. She gave a great *whew-w-w* of relief and, in her abbreviated night attire, bounded out of bed. "Come on, little peoples. This is a wonderful, wonderful day. Kay and her husband and their little boy Jodey are coming today."

❧ 2 ❧

Beany plunged into her busy day, singing lustily. In the guest room she made up the bed, which opened out to accommodate two. For Kay and Joe. The love seat could be moved in from the living room to make into a bed for Jodey.

Her singing was halted momentarily by another happy thought. Maybe her sister Mary Fred and her young doctor husband would be driving down from Big Basin in Wyoming today also. Mary Fred had always been the equestrienne in the family, and Miggs had arranged for her to keep her bay horse while the Johnny Malones were in Texas. No *maybe* about it, Beany remembered further. This was Wednesday, and the day Dr. Ander Erhart didn't have office hours. Whenever the Erharts had business in Denver, they came on Wednesday. There would be a joyous reunion around the dining table at the Buells' tonight.

Beany hurried to take two fryers out of the freezer. She remembered Kay's fondness for chocolate. She found a cake mix in the cupboard and—this was her lucky day!—a package of chocolate frosting. She said to an imaginary Kay, "Yes, you can have the outside piece."

She was measuring the liquid for the cake when she had a sudden vision of a red-cheeked girl laughing so hard she spilled milk over the glass cup they used in the cooking lab at Harkness High. McNally. Her first name was Linda, but because there were five Lindas in their class, they were all called by their last names. And because Beany's name began with *M* (she had been Malone then) and Kay's with *M* (for Maffley), McNally, Maffley, and Malone had always been grouped together in lab work or gym.

McNally was short, and a little on the plump side, and when she laughed—which was often—she laughed all over. Beany, here in her own kitchen, chuckled at the memory.

She had another swift vision of McNally walking across the university campus or sitting in the Student Union, and looking up with adoration at the tall engineering student whose fraternity pin gleamed on her red slipover. McNally was partial to red.

On a sudden impulse Beany reached for the phone book. It would be wonderful for the three of them— McNally, Kay, and Beany—to get together. Even as she dialed, Beany remembered reading in the paper about the McNally parents being in an automobile accident last summer. She had meant then to get in touch with McNally. But two things had put it out of her mind: Carlton's father had died suddenly from a heart attack, and at the same time Mary Liz was having trouble with her formula.

Her phone call went unanswered. "I'll try again this evening," she vowed as she slid the cake into the oven.

She took a moment to look at the scuffed living-room floor and regret that as yet only a few small rugs made an unsuccessful effort at covering it. For they were now so limp from washing, they neither lay flat nor stayed in place. "Our scatter rugs are skittery ones," Beany admitted.

Another old school friend, Dulcie Trighorn, could never resist crowing over her because she, Dulcie, had all new furniture in her house long before Beany had much beside the love seat—a wedding present from her stepmother—and a few cast-offs from here and there. Dulcie never missed a chance to say, "Bare floors look like poor white trash to me. *When* are you going to get a carpet?"

"That'll be next, now that Mary Liz is paid for."

How unstretchable dollars were! Beany and Carlton had been married four years, and for two of those he had been finishing law school. But now the fund was started for the oval rug Beany had set her heart on. Every time she saved a few dollars on household expenses, or Carlton managed a little extra over their regular payments, the money went into a jewelry box that played "In the Gloaming, Oh, my darling" when the lid was lifted.

Kay is coming back. Beany wanted to shout it from the housetops. Instead she phoned. Her stepmother,

Adair, was a painter, and her first comment was, "Ah! our sweet Kay. I wonder if she still paints. Remember how she wanted to do a sort of Chagall 'Lovers in August'? You know, the one with the bouquet in the foreground and a couple embracing in the misty background? Only Kay wanted to have a peach tree in blossom in the foreground and a couple dancing in the background."

"That was because she and Joe danced at a pavilion in a peach orchard during their whirlwind courtship."

Beany phoned Dulcie next. Dulcie said, as though her mind were on something else, "So Kay and Joe and their little boy are coming. He's about a year older than our Gussie. Beany, do you know how much it costs to resilver an old coffee pot? Mom offered me one that had been her mother's when I got married, but it looked so tacky to me then—"

Dulcie and her one-track mind! Beany answered shortly, "You can call a silversmith and find out," and hung up.

The children were napping that afternoon, and the inconstant sun was again lost in a gun-metal sky, when Beany went out to their mailbox at the curb. She was looking through the mail when the first visitors arrived in a gray station wagon with a Wyoming license and a horse trailer attached.

Mary Fred climbed out of the car, but her husband in his wide-brimmed hat called out to Beany that he would go on to the farm and load up the bay horse, and then come back and reload Mary Fred.

"But you'll be staying for supper?"

Mary Fred answered for both of them as he drove on, "Of course. Don't we always plan on a good meal at the Buells'?"

Mary Fred Erhart was three years older than Beany. There was a strong family resemblance between them. They both had the same wide mouth that was made for smiles. And the same gray-blue eyes, put in with what the Irish called "a dirty finger," meaning with dark lashes and brows. How Beany had lamented in her teens that the same dirty finger had sprinkled freckles over her nose and cheeks!

Beany told her the news about Kay, and Mary Fred said, "Little old Kay! It'll be good to see her. I wonder if Joe is still so handsome—so like all the all-America athletes rolled into one."

"He was so devoted to Kay—Cooky, he called her. Remember how anemic she was before the baby was born, and how Joe would carry her up the stairs to the rooms over our garage where they lived," Beany mused. "I think she's had trouble with anemia ever since. Because when I asked her to send a snapshot, she said she looked too washed out to pose, but that she was gulping down builder-uppers."

"Is Kay's flibbertigibbet mother still in Peachtree?"

"Oh, no! There's only Kay's grandfather Jethro there now. Don't you remember Kay's mother went to Hawaii before Kay and Joe were married?"

"I don't remember where she went, but I remember her sending Kay and Joe those ornate silver candlesticks for a wedding present when the poor things didn't have a table to put them on," Mary Fred said.

"Kay certainly never got any *mothering* from her."

Beany smiled ruefully. "She was so vain. She didn't even want to be called mother—she wanted people to call them Kay and Fay. She told about someone calling them the Winsome Twosome. Johnny used to call them the Gruesome Twosome."

The front door, which Beany hadn't closed tight, was pushed open by Mary Liz. A light sleeper, she had evidently heard their voices. She came toddling down the flagstone path and, sure of her welcome, made straight for her aunt's arms.

Mary Fred swooped her up. "Well, look at you in your pink peignoir, and smelling like what I think mignonette smells like."

"It's the robe from Kay. I had to put it on her last night, and now I can't get it off her. I keep wondering why the Collinses are coming. Do you suppose they've worked it out so Joe can go back to the university? Their little Jodey will be five in September," she added.

Beany carried the mail into the house while Mary Fred carried in her niece. She dropped down on the love seat and said accusingly over Mary Liz's pink shoulder, "It isn't fair, Beany."

The times, the times, Mary Fred had announced, "My idea of happiness is a stableful of horses and a houseful of kids." She had the stableful of horses. It was on the Erhart ranch, twelve miles from Big Basin where Ander was an assistant to an older doctor. The stableful consisted of Mary Fred's two palominos and Ander's sturdy roping horse. Now Miggs's bay would fill another stall. But there hadn't been even a start on the houseful of kids.

16

"Mary Fred, the idea! Give yourself time," Beany said.

"Time? I've been married over two years. It didn't take you even *one* to bring forth Mister."

Mister himself emerged from the bedroom and sat on the floor to put on his shoes. "Don't tell me whichever foot whichever shoe goes on. I don't like people to tell me."

His mother and aunt winked at each other. Mister had that rare trait in a child of being sober and thoughtful and, at the same time, so happy and contented that he sang himself to sleep. He had never prattled baby talk as his volatile younger sister did. He seemed to turn words over in his mind and then to use them slowly and correctly. Beany often found herself explaining something to him as though he were an adult instead of a responsible little three-year-old.

His name was James William, but he had acquired the name Mister by one of life's small quirks. The ice-cream man, seeing him quietly waiting his turn, in contrast to the other pushing and clamoring children, would always turn to him and say, "And what would you like, little mister?" The name had stuck.

The two sisters visited over cups of coffee, and through Mary Fred's coaxing Mary Liz out of the fleecy robe and into a handkerchief-sized T-shirt and striped pants. They visited on while Beany cut up the fryers, seasoned them, and put them in the oven.

There was much ado when Ander pulled into the side driveway with the bay horse in the trailer. Not only did the Buell two and Thumper have to go out and inspect this rare specimen called a horse, but children of all sizes seemed suddenly to bob up from side-walks and under bushes. Because Ander held Mary Liz and Mister up to stroke the horse's neck, every other child felt entitled to the same privilege.

He came in at last, short of breath and with his shirttail pulled out. Ander had left the Wyoming plains to attend medical school. Even with an M.D. after his name, he still entered and won calf-roping contests. He talked with a soft drawl and walked with a cowboy's rolling gait. His face was always tanned, and a myriad of sun wrinkles framed his eyes. His hands were slim-fingered, strong and capable; his eyes probing and alert. He was especially fond of and in-terested in children.

Beany poured him coffee, and then went to the door to call to some of the children not to climb onto the horse trailer. She stood in the doorway and watched them disperse. The laggard sun had come out from behind gray clouds to make a sunset splash over the mountains in the west.

She was about to close the door when she saw a car coming slowly down Laurel Lane as though the driver were looking for a certain number. Her heart started a glad thumping when she saw its Utah license. She said over her shoulder to the ones in the room, "This must be the Collinses now. Kay wrote me once about their getting a dark-blue convertible with red leather—Yes, it's stopping."

She ran out the door and across the lawn just as the mud-splashed and laden car stopped in front of their winding flagstone path. A man—yes, it was Joe Collins!—got out. He reached back for a smaller passenger who seemed reluctant to leave the car. Yes, that would be Jodey.

Beany called out as she ran toward them, "I've been looking for you all day. I've got your room all ready, and I baked a chocolate cake because I remembered—"

She stopped short. She was near enough now to see that no one else was in the car. She looked at Joe, and part of her mind registered that he was as handsome and broad of shoulder as ever, but looked much *older*. Of course! It had been four years since she had seen him.

"Where's Kay?" she asked.

She saw his features go lumpy. He turned back to the car and took out a well-wrapped package and thrust it at her. "Frozen cherry pies from the Collins' freezer plant. Kay thought maybe you'd—"

"But Kay said in the wire you were *all* coming."

The lumps came back into his face. "Yeh—yeh, sure, little old Cooky came with us. I brought her down to see a specialist. God's sake, Beany, I'd had enough of getting the old run-around from the doctor there. I heard about this specialist—Kostra. Do you know him?"

"I think I've heard of him. Is that why you came? But where—"

"Kostra took a blood count the very first thing. He rushed it through while we waited in the office. And then he—he isn't the kind to horse around—he plopped Cooky right into St. Michael's Hospital. I took her there and stayed until they ran me out."

A jolted Beany could only stare at the misery in Joe's face, and at the small boy, standing ramrod stiff beside his father. He had inherited Joe's broad shoulders, along with Kay's blond hair and morning-glory blue eyes.

She heard herself saying with a cheerful heartiness that didn't ring true even to her own ears, "Well, that's a good thing, Joe. I mean, in a hospital they can take tests and all that—and then they'll prescribe whatever she needs to bring her blood count up. Nowadays they put people in hospitals just so they can rest and build up. Come on in, both of you. You're just in time for supper."

She reached out a hand to the little boy, but he backed away from her and clung tighter to his father.

❦ 3 ❧

Inside the house, when Joe had been greeted by Mary Fred and Ander, he repeated his story of the doctor's putting Kay in the hospital. He looked so jittery and haggard that Ander said, "Beany, I'll bet Joe could stand a drink," and Joe breathed, "I sure could, Beany, if it's handy."

She reached into the cupboard for the bottle she always thought of as Uncle Matthew's. Just as the cup of coffee was a near ritual with him in the morning, so was his "two fingers of Scotch" on his stopover after work in the evening.

Ander took the bottle from her and mixed a drink. He asked as he handed it to Joe, "What was Dr. Kostra's diagnosis of Kay? Or did he say?"

"I couldn't get much satisfaction out of him," Joe grumbled. "He said he wants to call in another doctor for consultation, and take more lab tests."

He took a deep draft from the glass in his hand, and launched into a bitter diatribe against the doctor in Peachtree. "That old mossback, with his tonics and liver shots! Cooky's been fighting this weakness for years."

Beany shakily stirred up an orange drink for the children. She carried a glass in to the woebegone little boy who stood watching the whole scene with distrustful eyes. "Here, Jodey, I'll bet you're thirsty."

"No," he said, shrinking away from her.

"Can't you say, 'No, thank you, Mrs. Buell'?" his father said automatically. He explained to the rest of the room, "We planned to leave him with my sister— she's got four of her own—but at the last minute he raised such a holy ruckus, there was nothing to do but bring him. He never wants Cooky or me out of his sight."

Beany pushed up a child's low stool. "Sit down here, honey, next to your dad."

"No," Jodey said again.

"He's been sitting in the car all day." Joe said excusingly. "We couldn't get him within shooting distance of the hospital." He reached out and ruffled the boy's light hair with a fond grin. "How we doing, buckaroo?"

Some of the poker-like stiffness left the child. He crept closer to his father so that their shoulders touched. He made no response to Mary Liz's, "Hi," which she repeated until her aunt drew her away with a murmured, "Never mind, he's tired." And no response to Mister's generous offer, "If you want to pet our dog, I'll hold him for you," except a challenging, "I'm bigger'n you."

Thumper's whimpering at the door told Beany that

the man of the house had driven up. She stepped out the door and looked with trepidation toward the car. But Carlton was already out on the driver's side, and Uncle Matthew was sliding over under the wheel.

Beany waved at him. He was taking longer than necessary to settle himself for the short drive ahead. She knew that he was giving her time to call out, "Come on in, Uncle Matthew, and meet these friends of ours."

But if she did, he would take the floor and hold it, as she well knew from past experience. He wouldn't stay for dinner—"Thank you, Beany, my dear, but Ruth is expecting me"—yet he would stay on and on until the guests fidgeted in boredom and Beany was in near panic over how her dinner was standing the delay.

She briefed Carlton on the doctor's hurrying Kay into the hospital. "So only Joe and little Jodey are here."

Inside, Carlton exchanged warm greetings and handshakes with their guests. He put out his hand to Jodey with a "Good to see you, son." Children liked Carlton with his unpatronizing acceptance of them. But Jodey ignored the proffered hand and said with his deadpan expression, "My dad's bigger'n you."

"That's right. And a lot stronger, too."

Joe said uneasily, "Right now he's got a thing about who's bigger than who. I don't know what he's trying to prove."

Strange how shock and concern befuddle the hands as well as the head. Beany moved through the supper preparations, confused and clumsy. Mary Fred was a willing but inept helper. In their school days when Mary Fred took her turn at cooking, she leaned so heavily on meat loaf that their brother Johnny insisted that his wife would not only have to vow, "I promise to love, honor, and obey," but add, "and never, never, cook meat loaf."

This evening, as always, Beany shook up her salad dressing in a pint jar. But this evening she tipped it over and spilled most of it. While she was wiping it up, the rice that was to be served with the chicken stuck and scorched.

It all seemed so *un*right. For Kay's husband and child to be here in her house, and Kay in a hospital room. So *un*right for a small boy with Kay's blond hair and blue eyes to shrink away from her, Beany. Because it hurt her to look at the cake with chocolate icing, she asked Joe, "Can I go over to the hospital with you this evening, and take Kay a piece of cake?"

He shook his head unhappily. "The doctor is giving her something to make her sleep. He said that the five-hundred-mile drive from Peachtree was pretty hard on her. He told me to wait till tomorrow to go and see her."

The Buell ranch house was laid out so that there was little privacy in it. The front door, which was painted turquoise to match the shutters, opened into a small hall. A step to the left took one into the kitchen; a few steps straight ahead, into the living room. One end of it was given over to dining table and chairs; French doors opened out of it onto the patio and back yard—and the clotheslines where part of Beany's wash still hung, limp and damp. Only a half partition, breast-high on Beany, separated the living and kitchen areas.

So that all the while Beany was fumbling through the meal-getting, she heard Joe Collins railing on and on about the doctor in Peachtree. But when she attached the cord to the percolator, he had switched to his cousin Keith Collins, who now ran the bakery and freezing plant in Peachtree and was Joe's boss.

"Old big-britches Keith. If it hadn't been for him, I'd have brought Cooky down here to a specialist long ago. But it was always a bad time to leave, according to our boy Keith. Then when Cooky got those lumps on her neck and under her arms, I decided she needed more than the brown medicine that old horse-and-buggy doctor was giving her."

Beany's and Carlton's eyes met in understanding. *Poor Joe, taking out his shock and grief in ranting at whoever he could find to rant at.*

Ander and Mary Fred, with the long ride ahead of them, left as soon as supper was over.

And then Kay herself telephoned from Room 208. Joe turned from the phone to relay to Beany and Carlton, "She says she's feeling a lot better, and she cleaned up everything they brought her on her supper tray. She wants to say hello to you, Beany."

They said more than hello. Kay asked about everyone. Beany told her of Johnny's moving to Dallas because of a well-paying TV offer. And of Mary Fred and Ander coming down and taking the bay horse back to Big Basin with them.

"How is Jodey?" Kay's voice was suddenly anxious.

"Just fine. Our Mister let him sit on his high stool at the table, and you should hear Mary Liz, with her limited vocabulary, carrying on a conversation with him."

All this was a gross exaggeration. Mister hadn't *given* him the stool. Jodey had snatched it from him, and it had taken much diplomacy from Carlton to convince Mister that a volume of Bartlett's *Quotations* on another chair was slightly superior to a high stool. And the conversation Mary Liz carried on with Jodey had been completely one-sided with his lips clamped tight.

But the exaggeration was worth it to hear the relief in Kay's voice, "Oh, I'm so glad. He's going through some sort of phase—well, I'll tell you more about it when I see you."

And so the bed in the guest room sufficed for Joe Collins and son, and there was no need to make the love seat into one.

From the hall of the ranch house, a right-angled turn took one down the hall. On one side of it was the children's room and a large walk-in storage closet; on the other, the guest room and the bath. At the end of the hall, and running the width of the house, was the more sizable bedroom, known as the master bedroom, though there was little room to spare when the king-size bed, a chest of drawers, and vanity were set up.

Beany had been brought up in an older, wide-bosomed, two-story brick house where thick walls and snug doors shut out sound. Not so in this ranch house of clapboard. Even though the door of the guest room was closed and Beany was in bed, she could hear Joe patiently reassuring Jodey that nobody needed a light on when he went to sleep.

"Don't turn it out," Jodey kept saying.

Joe didn't. Beany could see the light splaying out the front window onto the lawn, and she thought, Joe oughtn't to humor him that way.

She was dozing off to sleep and was but dimly conscious that the light had gone off in the guest room. Joe had evidently waited until the little boy fell asleep to turn it off.

Beany suddenly jerked upright in bed. Jodey was screaming, "It's dark—it's dark—" There was such stark terror in the scream that her one longing was to race down the hall to him, cradle him in her arms, and say, "Don't be afraid. Nothing can hurt you."

Carlton laid a restraining hand on her. "He's all right, Beany. Joe's with him."

They both heard Joe's reassuring rumble again as the light went on.

Mary Fred and Ander drove north with the trailer and its occupant rolling smoothly along behind. Mary Fred carried on the conversation.

For several years before her marriage, she had kept her two palominos on the Johnny Malone acreage. Her two had shared the same pasture and stable with

Miggs's bay, Shandy. Mary Fred wondered if they would recognize each other and resume horse relations. She talked then of how she would have to exercise the bay as well as her own Sir Echo.

"Shandy's mouth is hard as shoe leather," she thought aloud. "He's more of a handful than Sir Echo."

Her other palomino was Sir Echo's mother, Miss Goldie, a gentle mare with soft, brown eyes and loving spirit.

They were far out on the plains before Mary Fred talked herself out. They rode on in silence with Ander never taking his eyes off the ribbon of road, except when he lowered them to the mirror to check on the hulk of dark horse in the trailer behind.

When the silence stretched on and on, Mary Fred touched his arm. "Come back, come back, wherever you are."

He turned his eyes toward her, and she realized with a small shock that he had indeed forgotten she was there. "I was thinking about Kay. She's in far worse shape than Joe realizes—and maybe it's just as well. Did you hear him mention the swollen glands in her neck and axilla?"

"Yes. What does that mean?"

"Along with her weakness and faintness, only one thing—leukemia."

They rode along in grave silence for a mile or two before he added, "And I can't get little Jodey out of my mind."

"I was thinking about him, too. Do you suppose it's

because Kay has been weak and ailing and not able to crack down on him? But did you ever see a more spoiled brat?"

"It isn't that," he said sharply. "Though I'm sure that's the conclusion everyone will jump to. No, there's something inside him—I don't know what."

"He was probably upset about his mother having to be in the hospital."

"That, yes. But I have a feeling it goes deeper than that."

❧ 4 ❧

The next morning Joe Collins, with nice courtesy, kept himself and little Jodey out of sight until Uncle Matthew had been given coffee, listened to, and had then departed with Carlton. For that, Beany was thankful.

Joe was planning on leaving his car at a garage to have the transmission checked. "I'll see if there's one near St. Michael's—near enough so I can walk. And I want to find her a pair of those fuzzy, fur slippers —lavender, I hope. You know how she likes anything purple?"

Later when he opened the door to leave, he told Jodey who watched with stricken eyes, "You play with Mary Liz and Mister till I come back."

"I want to go with you."

"Not today, buckaroo. I've got to cover too much ground. When I come back, I'll bring all three of you little fellows a surprise." On that, he went out the door.

There was no screaming tantrum from the little

boy. He glued himself to the screen door, looking after the black convertible and saying, "I want Dad. I want Mommie."

"Come out in the back yard with me, Jodey, while I get the clothes off the line."

Beany reached for his hand, but he dodged away from her and, like a little rabbit running for cover, made for the couch in the living room. Almost quicker than the eye could see, he tumbled over the back of it.

The couch was set slantwise in the corner. Mister bent over the back of it to say encouragingly, "You can roll up some of the socks. I'll show you how." He was told, "Go away." Mister, the literal-minded, did.

But Mary Liz made a hilarious game of Jodey's position. She would peer through the crack at the side and say, "Peek," and pull back and laugh delightedly. Beany listened for Jodey's "Go away." He didn't say it, but neither did he join in the game.

She left them and went out to the sunny back yard and her clothes whipping gaily on the line. The socks, big and little and of every color in the rainbow, she could hand to Mister, and he would mate them; he even painstakingly rolled each pair into a ball the way she had shown him.

She wheeled her clothesbasket through the living room and into the service room. She pulled Mary Liz away from the TV and her twisting of dials. "I'll turn your program on for you. Jodey, did you ever watch Romper Room?"

"Gone," said Mary Liz.

"Who's gone?"

"Jodey gone."

Beany took swift inventory behind the couch. She even looked under it, although Jodey would have to lie awfully flat to be there.

"Where did he go, Mary Liz?"

"Gone."

He must have decided to take refuge in another part of the house. Beany looked first in the room he had slept in last night with his father. And then in the children's room, the bath, the hall closet, in her and Carlton's room with its wide bed. Her heart thumped harder each time she got up off her knees after peering under a bed.

There was no place else a small boy could hide in a very unprivate, one-floor ranch house. No place in the kitchen, although Beany in mounting panic opened the lower cupboard doors. No place in the service room with its washer and ironing board. She raced through the door into the garage. But it was silent and empty except for Carl's old and cumbersome station wagon on the oil-stained cement floor, cartons lining the sides, paint buckets on shelves, and yard implements hanging on the walls.

She ran outside, and looked up and down the street. No Jodey was in sight, but a neighbor two houses down was setting her hose, and she called out, "Beany, are you looking for a little boy in a green T-shirt?"

She nodded, and ran down the walk to her.

"I just came out to turn on the hose when he came by like a fast freight. I didn't see where he came from —and I didn't recognize him—"

"Which way did he go, Dotty?"

Dotty pointed north, which was the direction of downtown. Beany's two children also came tumbling down the sidewalk, and her neighbor said with suburban helpfulness, "You go ahead, Beany, and I'll keep your two here. Go on, before he gets run over—or no telling what."

Beany ran. Thumper left the children and leaped joyously beside her.

She made the mistake of covering the first long winding block at too fast a pace. But she couldn't wait to reach the corner and see which way he had turned. She saw him a long block ahead of her—that blob of green shirt, and the towhead. Without an instant's wavering on his part, and as unerringly as a dog on the scent, he took the turn Joe's car must have taken to get him onto the main thoroughfare going toward town.

She was too far away to call, even if she had the breath to. Besides, she had a feeling he wouldn't wait for her, much less turn and come back. So she ran on. Jodey took another turn, and so did she. She would slow to a walk and then break into a trot. She was gaining on him. He seemed to have no thought of being followed; he never looked back.

These long, ambling blocks in suburbia! At last, Beany had shortened the distance between them enough to call out, "Jodey, Jodey, stop!" He turned and saw her and the dog, and ran on faster. She, too, increased her speed, calling frantically, "Jodey, wait for me."

A truck was stopping at one of the houses ahead of Jodey, and two workmen in white coveralls climbed out of it. They halted on the sidewalk, taking in the situation of the fleeing child and pursuing young woman calling at him to stop. The older and more heavyset of the two men blocked Jodey's passage and caught him by the arm.

There was nothing submissive about the boy. He fought, flailing and kicking. Evidently some of his kicks landed. Beany, as she reached the threesome on the walk, saw the marks of Jodey's wet and muddy shoes on the man's white pants. He gave him a hard shake, along with a threatening, "Cut that out, you little whelp."

Beany could only pant for breath, noting that the pale yellow truck at the curb was lettered, "Day-Nite TV Service. TV Tubes Checked in Your Home. Free Estimates," and that the man holding Jodey at arm's length had the name "Curt" in red stitching on his pocket.

He challenged Beany, "This your kid?"

She shook her head, managed to gasp, "His mother —is in the—hospital. He was—trying to—follow his dad."

Jodey spoke for the first time, "I want Dad."

"If you ask me," his holder volunteered, "he wants a good blistering. He's old enough—what is he, about five?—to know better than to go pelting down the street and across intersections, hell-bent for leather."

"It's been an upsetting time for him," Beany said. She thanked him again, smiled shakily at his younger helper, and, her arm tight on Jodey's arm, turned toward home. He didn't resist. She said on a ragged breath, "Jodey, you shouldn't run away like that."

"I want Dad. I want Mommie." It wasn't a childish wail, but a statement of terrible desolation.

"Of course, you do. I'll tell you what, Jodey. I'll find someone to stay with Mister and Mary Liz this afternoon, and I'll take you to see your mother."

"Will we bring her home?"

"I don't think so. The doctor wants her to stay there awhile and get better. But she'll be so glad to see you." And surely, a visit with his mother would allay his lonely anxiety.

The April sun was warm on her bare head when she stopped to gather up her own two from Dotty.

When the Buells first moved into this suburban area called Harmony Heights, Beany had been warmed by the friendliness of her neighbors. Constant lending and borrowing went on. An electric skillet, eggs, power mower, clinical thermometer, suntan lotion; a neighbor across the street, who traded baby-sitting with Beany, had even borrowed her love seat when she entertained her sorority.

But at times, such as this morning, Beany wished that neighborly curiosity wasn't also a part of suburbia. For Dotty felt entitled to know all about Jodey's mother, and how long Jodey would be in Beany's care. "Are you sure he's normal, Beany? He has a funny look in his eyes."

She was glad to see a pickup truck stop in front of her house and a man, woman, and child alight from it, so that she could say, "There are some friends at our house. Thanks, Dotty, for watching the children for me," and hurry off with Mary Liz scooped under her left arm while her right hand kept its firm grip on Jodey. Mister followed more slowly with a caterpillar on a leaf.

The man who came down the walk and took Mary Liz into his well-muscled arms was August Trighorn, husband of the Dulcie who yesterday had seemed more interested in having a coffee pot resilvered than in Kay's coming to town. He was called August only by his mother and father. Dulcie called him Trig, as did his fellow workers at the Bartell Bottling Company, where he was foreman.

His own little girl was close at his heels. Dulcie had said once to Beany, "You know, when we read that Lancelot and Elaine bit at school—about how pretty she looked floating down the river—I decided right then that when I had a little girl, I would name her Elaine."

And so she had—Elaine Augusta. But, alas, there was nothing about the child that even remotely resembled the Lily Maid of Astolat. She had straight hair, thin face, and alert, unblinking eyes. Dulcie, with disarming frankness, confessed to Beany, "I don't know why I had to get stuck with a homely kid like that." Elaine Augusta soon became Gussie or Gus.

This morning she was carrying a hammer, which she brandished proudly in front of the other children. "Lookit, lookit. It's mine."

36

"She takes it to bed with her," her mother said in disgust.

Dulcie, her blue eyes accented by makeup, her hair the color of burnt sugar, and her curves showing to advantage in orange slacks and black turtleneck, was a bright bird of paradise.

Yet, as Beany knew, Dulcie acquired her bird-of-paradise plumage at less than others paid for drab covering. She was deft with a needle. She could pick up a remnant from a basement counter for maybe $1.87, and two days later, people would exclaim, "That's a honey of an outfit."

Dulcie's eyes were on the small boy Beany was guiding toward them. "Look, Trig. He's got Kay's blond hair and Joe's football build."

"Are they here, Beany?" Trig asked.

She briefly explained the situation while they both listened in sympathy. Dulcie stepped over to Jodey, who had pushed close to Beany. "You're a year older than Gussie. Let's see how much taller—"

But as she reached out to him, he stiffened and shrank even closer to Beany. "No. No. Go away."

"For Pete's sake, I won't hurt you," Dulcie said, adding to Beany with a meaningful shrug, "Don't Kay and Joe believe in teaching a kid a few manners?"

Beany changed the subject. "What are we standing out here for? Come on in, and have a cup of coffee."

This time when they were all inside, Beany took precautions. She not only closed the front door but slid the night latch on. The French doors, opening onto

37

the patio and back yard, were no problem. The yard was fenced on the back and on one side. A thick hedge grew between their yard and their neighbor's on the south.

Beany put on the teakettle for instant coffee, and found a jar for Mister's caterpillar. Trig brought in Bartell's soft drinks for the children. Dulcie said as they sat down in the living room, "I was hoping you'd have your carpet by now."

. . . Many years ago Mary Fred, who had majored in psychology, had enjoined Beany, "Every time Dulcie riles you to the exploding point, just remember how she grew up. An itchy-footed father always chasing after the pot of gold at the foot of the rainbow—"

"Not gold, uranium," Beany had corrected.

"Just remember," Mary Fred had gone on unheeding, "all the years Dulcie was the shabby little new girl in school. So it's no wonder she likes to lord it over anyone she can." . . .

Beany, remembering, said equably, "Come fall, barring hell or high water, we should have it." She handed out coffee, and Trig opened bottles for the children.

Dulcie was talking about her Dames' Club. Beany had heard about it before. This bridge club was composed mostly of wives whose husbands worked at the big Durban Missile plant in North Denver where the Trighorns lived. She said proudly, "They just asked me to fill in, and now they want me to join."

Beany scarcely listened. She had suddenly remembered her rash promise to Jodey to take him to see his mother. But child visitors were not allowed in hospitals. Surely there must be some way—

"We're going on over to my folks," Dulcie was saying. "I want to get that old coffee pot Mom promised me before Dad takes a notion to pawn it."

"I thought you didn't want anything old in your house," Beany reminded her. Dulcie's exact words, when Beany had showed her the antique love seat wedding present, had been, "You won't catch me taking anybody's old hand-me-downs."

"I still think new things are better. But some of the Dames have really old silver things—like teapots and cake plates. They seem to think they're *something*. Come on, Trig."

The Trighorn daughter was saying, "I want to show Jodey and Mister how to pound nails."

Trig gave Jodey, Mister, and Mary Liz his quiet smile. "When we come again, I'll bring hammers and nails for all of you, and show you how to nail boards together. Now we're going home."

❧ 5 ❧

Afternoon visiting hours at St. Michael's were from two to four. At a quarter to two, Beany maneuvered her car into the parking space in front of the hospital. For a minute, and before she even hunted in her purse for a coin for the meter, she let her hands drop heavily in her lap and breathed out, "Here we are, Jodey."

He gave her only an uneasy flick of blue eyes. But then he had no idea of all the phoning, explaining, and cajoling she had gone through after her glib promise in order to get him here to see his mother.

When Trig, Dulcie, and Gussie (with hammer) had left, Beany had tried to call Kay to ask if she was allowed to have visitors. The girl at the hospital switchboard told her that the doctor had ordered no visitors and no in-going phone calls for Mrs. Collins. "The nurse can call out, but only the husband or doctor can call in."

It took many phone calls to track down the busy and curt Dr. Kostra. Yes, he told Beany, his patient had mentioned that she wanted to see her old friend. "But don't tire her."

"Could you give me permission to take Mrs. Collins's little boy with me?"

He turned a little testy at that. He had nothing to do with hospital regulations. His advice would be to leave the boy at home.

Beany's jaw did not have squarish lines for nothing. She thought of another Harkness High classmate: Andy Kern, who had danced with her and had danced with Kay at school hops and who was now Father Kern. She dialed his number, and heard his familiar voice boom out, "Knucklehead! What are you up to and why? And how are the little ankle biters?"

"They're fine, Andy."

He had not only been the best dancer Beany had ever known, but also the biggest clown. Even now in his clerical black, you could always count on him to liven up a gathering if it turned dull.

She told him the whole story of Kay's being in the hospital, of Jodey's bolting down the street, of his tortured, "I want Dad. I want Mommie," and of her promise to him. "But you know hospital rules, Andy."

"Yes, but so do I know the Mother Superior at St. Michael's. I think I can soft-soap her—"

Beany's giggle interrupted. "If you can't, nobody can."

"Tut-tut, child, where's your respect for the cloth? I'll call you right back."

He called ten minutes later. "I had to let Mother Sebastian run on and on. If you ever want to know the why of that none-under-fourteen rule, just ask the old padre. But, yes, you can take the little fellow so that he'll be comforted. Mother said there were no communicable diseases afloat. You're to get there a little before visiting hours, and don't use the elevator because other visitors might get ideas about bringing little codgers themselves. The stairs are on the left of the main entrance. Go up to second, and Room 208 is only two doors—"

Again her giggle interrupted. "I feel as though I were about to scale the Berlin Wall."

He laughed with her before he sobered. "I always hoped life would deal gently with Kay. Tell her I'll ask God to put her in His hip pocket."

Next Beany had to find someone to leave Mister and Mary Liz with while she was gone. Teen-age baby-sitters were in school on a Thursday afternoon. Her artist stepmother, who sometimes phoned and announced, "I'm ready to make like a grandma if you need me," was now off on a week-long junket with Beany's columnist father.

Beany's dependable standby had been Carlton's mother when she and the Judge lived in the old Buell home on Barberry Street. But since the Judge's death, Mrs. Buell had been in Arizona with relatives. The dark-brick, ivy-covered house, which Dulcie called a mausoleum, was rented now to a university professor.

Next door to the Buells on the south lived a very busy Dr. Kincaid, his almost as busy wife, and an even busier teen-age daughter. But they were neighborly neighbors, and today when Mrs. Kincaid heard of Beany's problem, she said instantly, "I'll be working out in the yard all afternoon. I can hear through the window when Mister and Mary Liz wake from their naps. You go ahead and take the little boy to see his mother, Beany."

Having gone through all that, Beany now opened the door of the car parked in St. Michael's driveway and said, "Come on, Jodey. Want to put the dime in the meter for me? Mister likes to."

Jodey got out. He didn't take the dime from her, but stood rigid, staring ahead to the imposing building at the end of the entrance driveway, where cars were thickly parked. "It's a hospital," he accused her. "I don't want to go there."

"But your mommie's inside, and she—"

She caught him by the arm as he bolted in the opposite direction. There it was again—that outer rigidity that didn't hide the inner trembling. She had to hold him tight while she dropped the dime in the meter. She said, "Your mother will look up and see us, and she'll say, 'Oh, look who's—' "

"I want her to come home."

"We'll ask her when the doctor will let her come home."

She didn't relax her grip as they went through the wide glass doors or when, after taking a turn, they climbed the stairs. Beany found herself walking with furtive softness, and whispering, "This must be 208, Jodey— Yes, it is." She pushed through the door which was slightly ajar.

For a half minute the two visitors stood, abashed by the very impersonal whiteness and neatness and silence of the room. Its occupant was asleep in the white, smooth bed, which was tilted up at an angle. With her eyes closed, and in the high-necked, white hospital gown, the girl looked so *lost*. Beany breathed out a startled, "Kay—Kay—"

The blue eyes opened. There was a melodic clink of bracelet, and identity was restored. She cried out on a gurgling intake of breath, "Beany! And my Jodey!"

The little boy broke away from Beany and ran toward her. But even as her arms reached out to him, he flung himself against the bed, beating on it and screaming out, "Get up! Get up! Come home—come home now!"

"Jodey, love— Jodey—" Kay tried to catch his thrashing hands with her thin, white ones. "Jodey, I'm coming home. Hush now, and listen. Just as soon as I can—"

"No, now. I want you to come home now."

The door was pushed open a little wider by a Negro nurse. Jodey looked up and saw her. He turned eyes of terror toward the door he had entered with Beany; the nurse's bulky figure blocked it. The door to the bathroom was partly open, and Jodey scurried for it. Once inside he slammed the door shut.

The nurse said, "I guess he's not used to seeing someone with a black face."

"Oh, no. It isn't that at all, Eudora. This is Beany I was telling you about. Beany, this is Mrs. Holden— the doctor thought I needed a *special* to poke all the pills down me—but I call her Eudora because it's such a pretty name, and besides it means *beautiful gift*. Oh, no, Eudora, it's your white uniform Jodey ran away from. He's scared to death of anyone in white. It started when he was in the hospital with his hurt shoulder. He just about flips if Joe even wears a white shirt. I had a white dress, and I had to dip it in blue dye because the poor little kid got so teed-off every time I put it on."

She was talking fast in excited happiness, "Beany, Beany, it's so good to see you. Tell me about you—and Carl—and your two. Oh, I wish I could see them. Stand in the light so I can see your freckled face better. I've missed you—I never get over missing you. Beany, was Jodey all right? I mean, he didn't act up or—?"

The nurse broke in—she had a low, gentle voice—"I'll leave you two to visit"; and Beany answered, "You run me out when I've been here long enough."

"Not too soon, please, Eudora," Kay called after her. She reached for Beany's hand and clasped it tight. "You don't think Jodey's a horrible brat, do you, Beany?"

Without waiting for an answer, Kay pulled herself up in bed, and began talking swiftly as though she had so much to say and not much time to say it in.

"You remember, Beany, we left Denver in May? Jodey was a year old that next September, and about Thanksgiving time he fell off the porch and broke his shoulder. It was all so terrible—he was knocked out, and Joe wasn't home—I mean he wasn't in Peachtree, because he'd gone with the football team to play their big Thanksgiving game. Grandpa Jethro and I rushed Jodey to the hospital, and they gave him an anesthetic and set his shoulder. I wanted to stay with him all night, but the hospital is little, and so crowded—Jodey was in a ward with three other children. And that was one of my worst weak and draggy times—"

"That's when you'd had a miscarriage, wasn't it?" Beany asked.

"Yes, and I would keel over in a faint at the drop of a hat. So Grandpa Jethro and I went over and got him the next morning." Her voice was uneven, almost shrill at times and then thinning to a thread.

"You mustn't tire yourself, Kay."

But Kay still had so much to tell her friend. "All of Joe's folks and Grandpa Jethro—oh, everyone in Peachtree—think I'm crazy when I say that Jodey's night in the hospital changed him. But, Beany, he'd never been away from Joe or me before. They all laugh and say thousands of one-year-olds have been in hospitals without any mother or father sitting there holding their hands. But, Beany, you remember what a good baby, what a happy baby, he was?"

"You bet I do. He'd always go to any one of us. Remember how he'd jump up and down in his crib and laugh?"

"But never since he came back from the hospital. He doesn't laugh—or cry either. I blame myself. If only I'd been able to take care of him, instead of being such a weak, anemic drip. If only we hadn't been living with Grandpa Jethro in his house. Grandpa sort of took over. I shouldn't have let him because his idea of bringing up children, especially boys, is just to paddle the living daylights out of them. Oh, the times I've heard him say, 'That kid has to learn to mind' or 'I'm

46

going to break him of running away.' Because—why, Beany, before the cast was even off his shoulder, that poor little tike started running away. But I don't think he's as bad as he was about it."

Wild horses couldn't have dragged it out of Beany that she'd had to chase Jodey six or seven long, winding blocks in Harmony Heights this morning. She said, "It's probably a phase he had to go through."

"Beany, you can see, can't you, that he isn't just a horrible brat that I—Joe and I—have spoiled rotten? Somehow I failed him—we all failed him. Joe's family mean well—I'm sure they mean well. They were always ready to take him off my hands so I could build up my strength. When Grandma Collins kept him, all she did was stuff him with ice cream and candy. And then Joe's sister—"

"Is she the one you planned to leave him with? The one who has four of her own?"

Kay nodded. "Aline. She's a bustler and a hustler, and heaven knows she has to be with all she has to do. She's always said that I humor Jodey too much, and that it wouldn't take her long to take the crimps out of him. A couple of times when she was keeping him, he ran away and she—she tied him to the clothesline—" A sob shook Kay's slim frame. "I went there—and there he was—just like a dog fastened to a leash—" She put her hands in front of her face and said chokingly through her fingers, "Oh, why did I have to be such a washout, so he was batted about with first this one and that?"

Beany dropped down on the bed and put her arms

around her. "Kay, please, don't blame yourself. Listen, honey, Ander Erhart says you've got the best specialist in town—your Dr. Kostra. He'll soon have you built up."

Kay's readiness to laugh! "That's what I told the doctor this morning, that a few more doses of his panther juice, and I'd be taking in floors to scrub. The happiest day of my life will be when I can tell Grandpa and all of the Collinses to go blow—With their blistering Jodey's behind and tying him to clotheslines. Then Jodey and I can play together the way we used to, and the old sweet and loving Jodey will come back. That's what I'd pray every night when he finally got to sleep: 'Come back, come back, Jodey, wherever you are. Come out of the dark. Come into the light.' "

"He will, Kay, he'll come into the light. I'll talk to Ander Erhart about him. He told me once that he had planned to go into child psychiatry. We'll all pull him out of the dark."

Again the door was pushed wider, and a nurse came in. This nurse was young, auburn-haired, and pert. It flashed through Beany's mind that she just missed being pretty, though she couldn't say why.

"Hello, Yvonne," Kay said. "I wondered if I'd see you when the doctor sent me here to St. Michael's. This is my friend, Beany Buell. Yvonne Plettner, Beany. She's from Peachtree, too."

"Are you on a case here?" Beany asked.

"Not me. I'm in the lab. And that's what I like. Believe it or not, I loathe nursing. I don't have any Florence Nightingale yen to soothe fevered brows. I guess I went into it because there wasn't much choice in Peachtree."

She grimaced as she talked, and she talked a lot. She stayed on, talking about someone from Peachtree named Dick, who worked in the lab, too, and who was married to a Betty Lou, also from Peachtree. At last she took her departure with the customary, "Glad to meet you, Mrs. Buell," and to Kay, "Let me know if I can do anything for you."

Kay waited until her footsteps receded, and then said on a laugh that was close to her bubbling, high-school one, "She'd be the last one I'd call on. And *I'd* be the last one she'd do anything for. She hates my guts. She was Joe's girl all through high school and up until he asked me to go to the senior prom. And then —Well, you know how it was."

"Your moonlight and peach-blossom romance. And you're still wearing your bracelet."

On the heavy silver chain, miniature gold and silver baseballs, basketballs, and footballs were attached, each ball not much bigger than a dried bean. They were all trophies won by Joe Collins, star athlete of Peachtree High.

"Jodey used to love to look at the little footballs and pick out Joe's name on each one. I always told him I'd give it to him when he was older. It's so loose on me now. Beany, do you suppose it would help him if I let him have it now—because you know how he worships Joe?"

"You keep it, Kay. It wouldn't seem like you without that little clink of background music."

Kay laughed softly, and pushed the bracelet farther up her arm. "No, Yvonne Plettner never forgave me for what she called my taking Joe away from her."

"No girl ever took a fellow away from another girl unless he was ready and willing to be took. I'll peek in at Jodey." Beany tiptoed over and opened the bathroom door and looked in. The little boy had drawn himself into as tight a knot as he could, and was in the farthest corner, which was a niche under the washbowl and further sheltered by the toilet.

"I won't come out," he told her.

"That's all right, Jodey."

Kay's laugh was rueful this time. "I'm glad Yvonne Plettner didn't know he was hiding in the bathroom. She was in training at the hospital in Peachtree when he was there with his broken shoulder, and I heard— you know how in a little town you hear everything— that she said he was the most hateful little monster that had ever been in the hospital."

"Could be sour grapes. Dulcie and Trig stopped in to see him this morning."

"Did Dulcie have anything to lord over you this time?" Kay asked it more in fondness than malice, for she had been on the receiving end, even as Beany had, of Dulcie's generosity.

"Oh, my, yes. *My* no carpet in the living room, and *her* Dames' Club." They laughed together in memory of Dulcie's bluntness and her bragging. Beany went on, "At first, I couldn't figure why she was so impressed by being in that club. But do you realize, Kay, that what with all her moving about, her working as a car-hop, her entering Harkness late and then not graduating, she has never before belonged to one? Most of us are run to death by them. I had a time cutting down to *one* book club and one church one."

Kay's nurse stood in the doorway, and they both exclaimed, "Is the time up already?"

"It was up long ago, but I heard you laughing, and I thought that would do Kay more good than medicine. I'll just step down the hall so the little fellow won't get upset again."

There was no further scene from Jodey. When Beany said, "Come on, Jodey, and we'll go home," he asked, "Will Dad be there?"

"He might be," she temporized.

He came out of his niche and took her hand willingly. "Wave to your mother," she coached him from the doorway. He waved woodenly, and Beany bent lower to hear what he was saying as they walked down the hall. It was, "Somebody's going to hurt her."

⚘ 6 ⚘

In the next two weeks Beany was in touch with Kay
every day. Joe took messages and the chocolate cookies
Beany made for her. Sometimes Mrs. Holden phoned,
and once or twice Kay did herself.

Beany visited her whenever she could get away. In
spite of the No Visitors sign on the door, she would
rap gently, and Mrs. Holden's grave eyes would light
up, and she would say softly, "Come in, Beany—come
in."

Two days after Beany's first visit, she had seen a
nightgown in a store window in the shopping center.
It was both glamorous and saucy, in shades of orchid
from very pale to deep purple, and all the widths
gathered onto a round neckline. With no thought of
the Buell budget, but only of how Kay loved those
shades and of how un-Kaylike she looked in the white,
tie-in-the-back hospital gowns, Beany bought it for her.
And reveled in Kay's girlish delight.

Another time, she took her a bouquet of peach blossoms which she had begged from a neighbor. Kay's

eyes misted over. "Oh, look, Eudora! Let's put them there on the window sill where Joe can see them when he walks in. And when I wake in the night, maybe the moonlight will be on them. Shove that big barge out of the way."

She meant a bouquet in a green boat-shaped vase. "Who sent the big barge?" Beany asked.

"Telegraphed from Hawaii," Kay said wryly. "Mother hasn't written a line—but that arrived."

She seemed far more pleased with a Get Well card from Father Andrew Kern and his scribbled, "May I have the next dance?" She was in high spirits that day and full of plans. She asked again about Johnny and Miggs and their moving to Texas. "How long did you say they'd be gone, Beany?"

"His contract is for a year with the TV company."

"And didn't you say nobody's living in their house?"

"That's right. We all love it, but it's just an old farmhouse with no central heating. Johnny calls the huge kitchen the foyer, library, beanery, and TV room."

Kay sat up in bed, her cheeks an excited pink. "When I get out of the hospital, would they mind if I lived out there with Jodey for a while? Joe will have to go back to his job in Peachtree. I worry about his staying away so long. But I don't feel up to going back until Jodey and I are both better able to cope with relations."

"Why, Johnny and Miggs would love to have you there. And I'll bring our two and come out on Strawberry Day."

"Strawberry Day!" Kay laughed joyously, and her bracelet fairly tinkled a melody. "Eudora, there's this big strawberry patch, and when they're ripe—"

"In June," Beany filled in, "and here it is May already."

"—why then Miggs's mother would have everybody out to pick them and to eat as many as they could hold while they were picking. And then after Migg's folks gave Miggs the farm when they got so rich with oil in Texas, Miggs kept on with Strawberry Day."

"Carl called it Stomach-ache Day," Beany put in again. "And this June *you* can have Stomach-ache Day, Kay."

"You'll come, too, won't you, Eudora?" Kay called to her nurse as she started out the door. Mrs. Holden always left Beany and Kay to visit together.

For only a second the nurse hesitated. "You bet I'll come, Kay," she promised.

"Won't Jodey love it?" Kay planned on. "Beany, is he a lot of extra trouble?"

"Not a lick of extra trouble," Beany lied.

Why tell Kay about Carl's buying a new lock for their front door and of his placing it so high to keep Jodey from reaching it that Beany herself had to stand on her toes to unbolt it? It was a worrying nuisance because now she couldn't call out, "Come in," to neighbors, the bread man, or dry cleaner. And one day when she left the door ajar, while she hunted for her purse to pay the newsboy, Jodey had darted out and down the street. The newsboy sprinted after him, caught him, and all but dragged him back.

To Beany's, "Jodey, why do you want to run away?"

she received only the barely audible, "Somebody's going to hurt me."

Beany told Kay instead, "Trig is going to bring over a folding cot for Jodey. It's one his brother had that isn't in use now. There's a big Trighorn family. So if you want anything, or want something done, Trig can either get it or do it, or knows someone who has it or can do it. Kind of an involved sentence—"

"But I know what you mean."

The next time Beany visited in 208, she found Kay looking drained and worried. "Trig brought the cot out," Beany explained, "and also Gussie with hammer, and also three dime-store hammers for our three, and also some scrap lumber for making a birdhouse. That's why I was able to get away. What's the matter, hon?"

"It's Joe. I love having him here, but I worry about his job at Peachtree. He hasn't written or phoned Keith. Oh, I know Keith is a feisty little know-it-all, and Joe isn't a bit happy there since Uncle Joe turned the business over to him. But after all he *is* Joe's boss —and after all it's a case of we need money, money, right now. Beany, see if you can get Joe to phone him and tell him why he's detained. Keith's the kind you have to butter up."

Beany nodded, and let her silence lie for her. The truth was that Joe had no job in Peachtree to save. Keith Collins, his cousin and manager of the freezing plant, had telephoned *him*. Even by rattling pans in the kitchen, Beany couldn't help hearing the angry explosion at Joe's end. No doubt there had been just as violent a one from Keith in Utah.

Joe had banged up the receiver, and walked the

55

floor venting his fury. "Can you imagine that little son-of-a-banty telling me to burn up the road and get back to the job or I wouldn't have a job to come back to?"

"But did you explain that Dr. Kostra was trying some new drugs on Kay, and that you wanted to wait and—"

"Thuh! What's a little thing like Cooky's living or dying to his packaging and freezing the crop of early peas? Do you know what I told him? I told him to keep his precious job."

But none of this could she tell Kay. She was even relieved when Mrs. Holden came back into the room, and Beany knew it was time for her to go.

At home, the sound of pounding reached her as she let herself in the front door. It came from the patio. She stood a moment, looking through the French doors at the absorbed workers. Trig was sawing and fitting the boards in place, and patiently showing each child where to pound a nail when his turn came. No golf playing for him on his one afternoon off a week.

At last, the birdhouse was hung from their cherry tree, which was just putting on its bridal froth and finery. Trig relaxed on the patio and drank a beer. He asked about Kay.

"They're trying some new drug on her. Today she was so worried about Joe staying away from his job in Peachtree that I didn't have the heart to tell her he no longer had a job there."

Trig to the rescue again! When the Collinses were in desperate straits before Jodey was born and Joe walked the streets looking for work, Trig had hired him to drive a Bartell Bottling truck. Now with warm weather coming on and the soft-drink business increasing, Trig said he could use another driver.

Joe took the job gratefully as he had five years ago.

He relayed to Beany, "Little old Cooky is full of plans about how maybe, come fall, I can work part time and go on to school and get the degree and the coaching job I always wanted. Yes, and she can't talk about anything but living out there on the farm while Johnny and Miggs are in Texas."

A few days later on a cloudy, chill afternoon that seemed all the more dour after days of bright sun, Mrs. Holden phoned Beany. Dulcie, with her small daughter, had stopped in at Laurel Lane to show Beany the coffee pot she had picked up at the silversmith's. When Beany put down the phone, she told Dulcie, "That was Kay's nurse. She said Kay was feeling pretty depressed, and that she felt chilly when she sat up. She said her negligee wasn't warm enough, and wondered if I had a soft sweater."

"Hold everything. I'll zip down to the shopping center and be right back. I've been wanting to send sweet old Kay something. You get out your sewing machine, Beany."

In half an hour Dulcie was back and unwrapping her purchases. Expertly she wielded the scissors over a terry beach towel with birds, flowers, and palm trees in vivid Gauguin colors. "I'll have this all stitched up and ready for Kay about as quick as you could hunt up a sweater."

And so she did, converting the towel into a bed jacket resembling a Mexican poncho, and bound all around with purple ball fringe.

"It's gorgeous, Dulcie. That will certainly lift Kay's spirits."

"Go ahead and take it to her so she can sit up in bed. If you won't be gone more than an hour, I'll stay with all four little hoodlums."

In the hospital room, Beany put the bed jacket on Kay, and Mrs. Holden wound her bed up to a sitting position and plumped the pillows behind her.

Kay tried valiantly to lift her spirits to match the gay garment. "Beany, I'm learning more about organs —only not musical ones. I'll bet you don't know where your spleen is."

"I didn't even know I had one."

"I know I've got one, and I can tell you right where it is." Her bracelet clinked in emphasis as she pressed her thumb into her left side. "I wish I'd been born without one."

Mrs. Holden said gently, "Dr. Kostra is sure this new medicine will take care of the swelling there."

"Then something else that I didn't even know I had will start acting up." What started as a laugh caught in her throat and turned into a sob. Beany took her hand, and Kay gripped it tight. "Oh, Beany, I want to get out of here—and take Jodey with me. I want to make up to him for all he's gone through. I keep think-ing of Grandpa Jethro taking a belt to him. And I couldn't stop him. Once I got out of bed and ran downstairs and grabbed Jodey away from him. And then—like a dumb dodo—I blacked out."

Mrs. Holden's voice chided, "Now, honey, don't be looking back. That's what Lot's wife did. And remember, she was turned to salt. You don't have to worry about how your little boy is being treated now—now that he's with Beany."

"He's just like one of the family, Kay. Joe keeps telling him to call me Mrs. Buell, but he hears Mister call me Mother, so Jodey calls me *Mrs. Mother.* And I just love it."

Kay's eyes begged for more news about Jodey. "And I told you about Trig and all of them making the birdhouse," Beany went on. "You ought to see the three of them, sitting and watching for a bird to fly through the round hole. The O-door they call it. When I left, Jodey was watching through our French door to see if a bird flew in."

She didn't add that when Dulcie came, he dived for his haven behind the couch. (Beany had moved it farther from the wall so that his quarters were less cramped.)

She sat beside Kay, talking on of little inconsequentials, until Kay's eyes grew heavy. Beany ceased talking, and Kay's blue-veined lids stayed closed. Soundlessly Beany stood up. Mrs Holden, who had stayed in the room today, followed her out the door and said in her low voice, "She had a bad night—I saw that by her chart. She'll sleep now. She's always more at peace when you've been here."

At home, Dulcie slid off the bolt on the front door to let her in. "You must have chewed the rag a long time with Kay. You've been gone almost an hour and a half."

"Kay loved your bed jacket." Beany mollified her. "I told her about your rushing out and buying the towel and whipping it up, and she said, 'Who but Dulcie would do something so wonderful?'"

Gussie was sitting on the love seat, her drowsy eyes on the TV screen. Beany glanced in both the small bedrooms. Her two were sound asleep in their cribs. The guest room was empty. She looked behind the couch. "Where's Jodey?" she asked.

Dulcie snapped, "There's no sense in your catering to that ornery brat of a kid the way you do. You don't have to—nobody has to. I don't have to, and that's for sure."

"What did you do to him?"

"I didn't do a thing to him. After you left, I told him he could either come out from behind the couch or I'd reach back and pull him out by the hair of his head."

"Dulcie, you didn't!"

"No, I didn't pull him out. Because he came out, and went out the French door there like a shot out of a gun. He hid himself down there by the incinerator under all those bushes. I wasn't about to go down there and get my eyes scratched out going in after him."

Beany stepped out onto the patio. The incinerator sat in the far corner of the yard, a square rectangle of smoke-blackened bricks largely hid by a thick growth of spirea bushes. Their branches, soon to be weighted down by white flower clusters, hung over almost to the ground, making a sheltered spot. Thumper had sought out that very place last summer when the days were scorching.

So the little rabbit, frightened by Dulcie's threats, had found a new woodpile to flee to!

Beany turned back into the house to say, "Dulcie, I know he's got all the earmarks of a spoiled brat. But Ander Erhart was down last Wednesday again, and he says he's emotionally disturbed—or what they call psychic damage—"

"Oh, flub and dub! And a lot of hogwash." Dulcie was rewrapping her silver piece. "Come on, Gussie." The little girl sat on in drowsy lethargy, and her mother added sharply, "On your feet when I tell you, or I'll psychic damage you."

When they were gone, Beany went out the French door again into the darksome day. Yes, who but Dulcie would generously rush into making an eye-catching bed jacket one minute and, in the next, callously threaten a little boy to pull him out of his hiding place by the hair of his head? Beany's stepmother had once said of Dulcie, "She's like a cow that gives a full bucket of milk and then puts her foot in it."

Beany walked down to the back corner of the yard and bent down to see the little figure with its blond head hunched over the drawn-up knees. "I'm looking for somebody because I'm lonesome," she said. "Mister and Mary Liz are still asleep, and Mrs. Twighorn and her little girl are gone, and I'm all by myself. I wish somebody would come in the house and drink tea with me."

About five minutes later, when she was putting the portable sewing machine away, she heard one of the glass doors open. Jodey did something he had never done before. He ran to her and threw himself against her, clutching her around the knees. She knelt and took him into her arms, crooning incoherent nothings to him. He was making strangling sounds but no words. Yet Beany had a feeling he was crying out, "Help me— help me."

❧ 7 ❧

The Bartell Bottling Company was as far to the north in the city as Harmony Heights was to the south, and Joe Collins's truck-driving job called for his reporting to work at seven each morning. He put in a week of driving from Harmony Heights to his job in the morning, back to the Heights when his day's work was done, and then, after showering and changing, taking another long drive to St. Michael's.

On Friday evening he told Beany he had rented a light-housekeeping room in a more central and convenient location. "I can move in right away."

"I'll go, too," Jodey said.

"Yes, you can stay with me if you're good, Jodey." For the landlady had told him that if he brought a cot and put it up, his little boy could stay with him. She was already caring for two of her grandchildren while their mother worked, and she'd be glad to earn the extra money Joe would pay her for looking after Jodey during the day.

"Did you tell her he was a—a little standoffish with people?" Beany asked.

"Yes, I told her he was apt to be a problem. But she said she had taken care of children all her life, and she had yet to find one she couldn't handle."

Joe thanked Beany for all she had done for them, and said earnestly it wasn't fair to impose on her further. He loaded into his convertible the Trighorn folding cot, a suitcase with his and Jodey's clothes, and a mesh bag holding the overflow. Jodey let Beany kiss him good-bye; he put his hand in Joe's and went off contentedly.

When the Malone-Buell nuptials had taken place four years ago, the groom's gift to the bride had been a fitted picnic hamper. "I know that, according to the book, the groom is supposed to give the bride something for the adornment of her person—"

"But not for picnic goers like us," Beany had assured him. "This will be for the adornment of our souls."

They called it the diamond brooch.

Mary Fred always said that Beany and Carlton started going on picnics in the spring when they had to scrape away snow to sit down. Here it was late in May, and they hadn't yet gone on one this year. They had been afraid to chance it with the running-away Jodey.

The next day, Saturday, they packed the "diamond brooch," bundled up the children, and headed straight for Gilfallon Park in the foothills, with its fireplaces, picnic tables, and closed pavilion for group picnics or dances.

It was like their courtship days with Carlton building a fire, boiling coffee when the flames flared high, and broiling steak when they flickered low. Almost, but not quite. For Mister dropped one of his shoes into the creek. Carl rescued it, and Beany propped it up by the fire where, instead of drying out, it caught on fire itself. And Mary Liz lost her balance and sat down so hard in the potato salad she broke the bowl. Beany removed the wreckage, but the rest of the day the two small Buells had eyes for nothing but the chipmunks and gophers industriously carting off the salad in small chunks.

As the sun sank low and the air turned chill, cars drove in and parked close to the pavilion. Beany lured Mister's attention from the fauna to the flora by giving him a small pine branch with cones on it. Before Carlton could finish repacking their car, several young people came hurrying toward them, calling out, "Oh, no, you Buells. You can't go home yet. You have to stay for our dance. We need a few more suckers to help pay for the hillbilly band and the beer."

The dance was put on by a group of young teachers who called themselves The Pedagogues, and who had been getting their teaching degrees at the university when Beany and Carl were going there. They were all young marrieds. Some had brought their small children because they had no one to leave them with. They all warmly welcomed Beany and Carlton and the two wide-eyed children.

A girl named Peggy who had been on Beany's swim team at the university caught her arm. Her thin face was burned a deep pink from a day in the sun, and she was noticeably pregnant. "How's your crawl stroke, Beany? Hey, I'll herd your two, and you go ahead and dance. Sit on my lap, little Bo-Beep, if you can find some lap." She pulled Mister up beside her on the plank bench that bordered the dance floor. "Where's your other shoe, toots?"

"Mother burned it up."

"Tch-tch-tch! Who'da thought it of *her*? This is my husband, Beany. Dance with him, too, so he won't be a wallflower with me." She sang out over Mary Liz's drooping head as they danced off, " 'Kick up a rumpus, but don't lose the compass.' "

Her husband laughed. "The next line is not 'Get me to the church on time,' but 'Get me to the hospital on time.' "

Beany hadn't realized how starved she was for dancing, laughter, music, and wacky talk. She told Carlton when she danced with him, "I feel so footloose and fancy-free. I don't even feel married."

"You don't, eh?" On the crowded floor they were jostled close to each other. He said, "Pardon me, if I seem to be squeezing you tight. It's purely intentional."

"Tch-tch-tch! Who'da thought I married a wolf."

Beany, checking on the children, found Mister still clutching his molting pine branch and trying to stay awake. Mary Liz was fast asleep on the scanty lap of Beany's one-time fellow swimmer. She asked as Beany squeezed down beside her, "Hey, whatever happened to McNally that used to be on our swim team? I tried to phone her to ask her to come to this shindig but no answer."

66

Whatever happened to McNally, who used to laugh all over?

"I've lost track of her," Beany said regretfully. "Remember, I was a college dropout."

"Yeah, yeah, you got your man after two years. I had to chase mine for three. And McNally went on for four and her degree. We both majored in kindergarten and primary. Did you ever hear of the Maria Godwin School down near the railroad tracks—you know, with a small petable zoo, and the kids plant onion sets to watch them grow?"

"Sure. My father wrote it up in the *Call*—about a year ago, I think."

"That's right. I forgot it was Martie Malone's piece I read. Well, this Maria Godwin was crazy about McNally when she went down for practice teaching. Maybe she's teaching down there now."

Beany remembered that special glow of McNally's when she walked on campus beside the tall engineering student. "Or maybe she's married. And then I read something in the paper about her mother and father being in a car crash."

The conversation was broken by Carlton's coming in search of Beany. "Go on, you two, and dance this before you wake up your family," Peggy, the expectant mother, urged. "I didn't think that corny band had it in them to play music like this. You look like the kind that ought to dance to it."

The music they danced to was "Some Enchanted Evening," and Beany sang as they danced in a special enchantment of their own.

They took their enchantment down the mountain with them and into their door where, with Mary Liz in Beany's arms and Mister in his father's, they warded off the overjoyed Thumper. They pulled off shoes and outer garments, and tumbled the half-asleep children into their cribs.

Carlton picked two pine needles from the few left on Mister's branch. He put them between his thumb and forefinger so that only the tips showed. "Take one," he told Beany. "Whichever gets the longer needle can stay in bed in the morning. Whichever gets the shorter has to oust himself out and shag kids and cook breakfast. Choose, Miss Footloose and Fancy-free."

The one she took was very short. "Looks like I'm the one to leap up and out when the sun's on the morn."

He *must* have quickly pinched the other needle in two. For he held up a still shorter one. "Nope. You get to sleep late like a kept woman. I'll even bring coffee to you in bed." His arms tightened around her and his nuzzling lips found hers. "Do you still feel *un*married?"

She laughed into his shoulder. "I prefer feeling married."

It was well that the Carlton Buells had their happy, carefree, honeymoon weekend. For late on Monday afternoon Joe Collins, still in his green denim uniform with "Bartell" lettered in orange across the back, and looking distraught and driven, brought Jodey, the folding cot, and the mesh bag full of his clothes back to the Buells'.

Joe had walked into a wrathful furor when he went to his rooming house after work. "There was some sort of fracas between Jodey and the landlady's granddaughter, and she says he bit her—the granddaughter, I mean."

"Where did you bite her?" Mister asked the culprit with interest.

"On her foot," he said in his deadpan way. "She put it in front of my little car when I was running it."

"The old lady was pawing the air," Joe went on. "She said I could stay but Jodey had to go. Maybe I can look around and find someplace else where somebody will look after him. Godsake, Beany, I hate to load him onto you again."

"Oh, that's all right, Joe." She reached out to Jodey who stood as ramrod stiff as he had that first day when the Utah car stopped and Joe said, "Cooky's in the hospital." But this time Jodey did not shrink away from her. She wondered irrelevantly if Joe's landlady would still say she had never found a child she couldn't handle.

Joe refused Beany's invitation to dinner. He wanted to change clothes, stop for a quick sandwich, and get to St. Michael's around five. Dr. Kostra had called in another doctor for consultation. "Kostra drops in to see Cooky after office hours, and I like to catch him and find out how she's doing. I wish he'd ever get down to plain facts, instead of all his medical gobbledy-gook."

He enjoined Jodey, "Now be a good boy for Beany. And I'll stop by in the morning and take you with me in the truck. Any time I'm not pushed on deliveries, I'll take you, buckaroo."

But when Joe went out the door, and Beany turned from her high reach to slide on the bolt, Jodey was saying on harsh indrawn breaths, "I want Dad. I don't want to sleep by myself."

"You won't have to," Beany comforted him. "We can put your cot in the same room with Mister and Mary Liz."

But here she ran into an unforeseen obstacle. This time it was the amiable Mister who said, "No. No, he can't sleep in our room."

All Beany's talk of Jodey being a guest, her explaining that he didn't like to sleep alone, would not swerve Mister. "He's mean to me, and I don't like him." Remembering Jodey's confiscation of the high stool, his constant "go away" to Mister's overtures, Beany couldn't in her heart blame him.

"Mary Liz, will you sleep in Jodey's room with him?"

And she, who had learned to say yes but not no, said happily, "Yes. With Jodey."

With the children more hindrance than help, Beany wangled Mary Liz's crib through the door and into the guest room across the hall. She made up the folding cot again for Jodey.

But there were still problems, as she and Carlton

found at bedtime. Mary Liz fidgeted in her crib and wanted a drink every five minutes. "It's the light," Beany said. "She's not used to sleeping with one on, and Jodey is terrified without it."

Carlton drove to the nearest drugstore and brought back a night light in the shape of a candle which gave off no more than a candle's glow. He attached it, and said firmly to Jodey, "Mary Liz is going to sleep here in the room with you. But you have to be nice to her. You have to take care of her. She can't sleep with a bright light on."

A long pause, and then a small voice said, "I'll take care of her. I'm not—afraid—not very much."

The other problem was Thumper. He had been used to sleeping between Mister's crib and Mary Liz's. Now he wasn't sure where his allegiance lay. He was still pacing back and forth between rooms when Beany went to sleep. In the morning she saw by the mussed rug that he had slept in the hall, halfway between the two rooms.

Three times in the next few days Joe stopped the huge, laden, and clanking Bartell truck in Laurel Lane. At the sound of it Beany would open the door through which Jodey darted. He would climb up into the seat with his father and be gone, sometimes for hours.

But that, too, came to a stop.

On a warm morning, just as May was coming to an end, Joe, again looking distraught and driven, brought Jodey back when they had been gone only half an hour.

Joe had unloaded his cartons of soft drinks at the Ragged Robin drive-in on the Boulevard. The inside waitress had asked him if he didn't want a cup of coffee as usual. He said no, because his little boy was waiting in the truck.

"So she said for me to bring him in, and she'd set him up to ice cream while I had my coffee. She was wearing one of those white nylon dresses, but I never gave it a thought. So I brought Jodey in and we were sitting in a booth when she came over with the ice cream. Jodey looked up at her, and by damn, Beany, he up and streaked out of there like a scalded cat. Godsake, I had to chase him through Boulevard traffic. He runs blind without ever looking."

"I know," Beany murmured.

"The waitress was burned to a nub. She said he knocked the dish of ice cream out of her hand, but I'm sure he didn't mean to." He gave a wry downtwist to his lips, "And you'd never guess what she said would cure him of acting like that."

Beany's smile was wry, too. "I don't have to guess. I know. A good blisterin'."

"So I brought him home because every stop I made I was afraid he'd bolt again." He tipped the boy's chin up to him. "Jodey, why? Why did you go tearing out of the Robin when the woman brought you ice cream? She was just being nice to you."

He made no answer. The blue eyes only took on the shrinking, haunted, somebody's-going-to-hurt-me look. Joe pulled him close. "I'm not mad at you, buckaroo. You come on out to the truck with me, and I'll give you that green drink you like. Come on, Mister and

Mary Liz, and pick out whatever kind you want. And, Jodey, you can carry a bottle in for Beany—okay?"

Whatever his faults, Joe's two redeeming traits made up for them in Beany's eyes: he was a loving, devoted husband to Kay, and a patient, understanding father to Jodey.

❧ 8 ❧

It was the last Saturday in May, and summer was here. Up and down Laurel Lane, husbands guided power mowers over lawns. Through their airplane hum sounded the snip-snip of pruning shears, children screaming, and neighbors calling back and forth.

Up and down Laurel Lane, barbecue grills were taken from their plastic shrouds and set up on patios. Last summer's swimsuits were hung on clotheslines to air, along with this winter's blankets which would be stored away. Storm windows were taken off, and screen doors put on. Suntan lotion, fly swatters, and extra ice trays were hunted up.

Carlton backed the old, cumbersome, but roomy station wagon out of the garage. He always used it for gathering up his Young America team for practice. Besides his work as a lawyer, he managed a community-center baseball team, composed of Italians, Mexicans, and Negroes, called the Bombshells.

Yes, summer was here. Down Laurel Lane came

74

the Pied Piper of today—the ice-cream man in his pink cart with its tinkling melody. Children came racing out of houses, clutching the nickels they had begged from parents.

The Buell two were among the racers. But an ice-cream cart was something new to Jodey, and therefore to be feared. He wouldn't go out. Mister brought him a frozen Popsicle.

A summer day and a happy one.

In midafternoon Beany's father and her stepmother, Adair, stopped by to take the children over to the park to see the baby ducks on the lake. "The mother duck sails out in the lead, and all the little ones follow behind in formation like a flotilla," she told them.

"I don't think they need any sales talk," Martie Malone said with his nice twinkle, for already Mary Liz was shouting, "Duck baby," and Mister, the more practical, was nudging his mother with, "Give us bread in a sack to feed the little ducks."

"Yes, but hold your horses until I give Grandma and Grandpa a cold drink."

Beany's neighbors often told her that her father and stepmother were the youngest-looking grandparents who ever came visiting in Harmony Heights. Martie Malone was a newspaper man; his column which appeared in their morning *Call* was also syndicated. He was a tall man who had never grown paunchy, and though his dark hair was peppered with gray, he walked with a springy step, and his eyes were both humorous and keen.

Adair was too young to be the mother of her step-

75

daughters, and she wore a smaller size dress than they. She was pretty and vital and had a ready laugh. Besides being a successful painter, she was a happy and understanding woman.

Both visitors stood looking around the Buell back yard. Martie's reportorial mind was probably choosing words that would best describe the sandbox and painted toys, the spirea bushes (Jodey's hideaway) now weighted down with white blossoms, and the cherry tree, losing its petals with each passing breeze.

Adair, the artist, was evidently seeing it in the colors it would take to put it on canvas, for she mused, "There's a lot of lavender in those white clusters."

Mister reminded them that it was time for their calling on the little ducks in the park. Beany hunted up her stale bread. Martie Malone asked, "You coming with us, Jodey?"

"No," he said, but his no wasn't as belligerent as formerly. He added, "Mrs. Mother said I could pick violets for her to take to Mommie at the hospital."

Alone in the back yard with him, Beany watched his towhead bend low over the clumps of green leaves and tiny purple blooms. He'd straighten up and hold one out. "See, a nice long stem so it can drink up water." (He was quoting her.)

In the kitchen she found a small, white pitcher to serve as vase. She was filling it with water when the phone rang. It was Kay's nurse, Mrs. Holden. "Beany, Kay said to call you. She thought maybe you could get hold of Joe right away for us. I tried at the place where he works—"

"What's the matter?"

"Kay is terri—pretty upset. She's just got a letter from her grandpa Jethro in Peachtree. She should have gotten it a couple of days ago, but the old gentleman didn't address it right."

"Has something happened to her grandfather?"

"No, he's all right. But in the letter he said that he was coming to Denver Saturday—that's today—and get the little boy and take him home with him. That's what's got her—all worked up." There was an interruption, and the nurse said, "She wants to talk to you herself."

Kay's voice was high pitched and shaky, "Beany, I've got to stop him. I should have got his letter days ago. He says he's coming down with a friend of his— I know him, it's a fellow named Brady. And he says he's going to take Jodey back with him. Listen to what he says, 'With you in the hospital and Joe working, Jodey needs a home and somebody to look after him. I'm sure he's wore his welcome out with your friend by now, and I know how that goes. Jodey's place is here at home with his own folks and not with strangers—' "

Beany put in, "That's crazy. We're not *strangers*, for heaven's sake."

Kay wasn't listening. She was saying, "I've got to get hold of Joe, and tell him to call Grandpa right away. He's got to call him before Brady finishes work, because that's when they'll start out. He's got to keep Grandpa from coming and getting Jodey." Her voice rose to a hysterical scream. "Beany, I'll get right out of this bed myself, and come out and get Jodey and hide out with him before I'll let Grandpa—"

"Kay, don't talk nonsense. Have Mrs. Holden phone his house in Peachtree, and *you* tell him that—"

"He wouldn't listen to me. He never did. I don't want him coming—"

"Then I'll phone him. What's his number?"

"No, no, it wouldn't do any good."

Beany was suddenly aware of Jodey still holding his bunch of violets. She motioned to the vase of water absently, watched without really seeing as he jammed the flowers into it, because she was hearing Kay's ragged despair, "Grandpa won't listen to you either. He thinks all women are stupid." Her voice was fraying out. "But if Joe told him—he'd listen to Joe—but Eudora says nobody knows—"

Beany could hear the phone changing hands, and now Eudora's firmer voice said, "I phoned Bartell's. And the girl at the switchboard said that, according to the route chart, Joe was off at three today."

Beany glanced at the clock, which said five minutes to four. "If I can't trace him on his route, I'll go over to where he has a room. But I'll phone Trig first. Tell Kay she's not to worry a minute about Grandpa Jethro getting his hands on—" because of her small listener, she finished with "—what he's coming after."

She hung up and phoned Trig at Bartell Bottling, and swiftly explained to him why she had to get hold of Joe Collins right away. Trig told her that Joe was off at three, but that he had offered to take an order out to a Young Democrat picnic at Oberlin Park.

"I'll tell you where I'm sure you'll catch him. At the Buckeye Bar and Grill. It's a long drive out to Oberlin, and he said something about stopping there for a sandwich and beer."

"Where is this Buckeye place?"

"It's right where Highway 40 cuts across North Broadway. It's the truck intersection. I'm sure they'll know Joe there, if you want to phone and leave a message."

"No, I'll drive over myself. I won't rest easy until I know Joe has phoned Kay's grandfather in Peachtree and stopped him in his tracks."

Heavens, she had almost forgotten the person most involved until he said, "I'm going with you to find Dad." She had forgotten, too, that she wouldn't be able to go anywhere without taking him because there was no one to leave him with. "Okay, Jodey, but we have to hurry. Grab your sandals, and you can put them on in the car."

She was well on her way before she realized he had not only brought his sandals but also the small pitcher of violets.

By getting on the straightaway, running north and south, Beany reached the Buckeye Bar and Grill in twenty minutes. She parked in front of it between a truck loaded with crates of spinach and a shiny blue Cadillac. She looked at all the parked cars. There was no sign of a Bartell Bottling truck. She hoped Joe hadn't come and gone.

With Jodey, she pushed through the swinging front door. One side of the large, square space was given over to booths and tables for serving food. On the other side was a horseshoe-shaped bar. The men who occupied its stools were mostly workmen. Beany was just wondering whom she should question about Joe Collins, when a waitress turned away from some customers in a booth and started past them.

She stopped short to stare unbelievably at Beany, and Beany stared back at the brown-eyed girl in a brown uniform and bright yellow handkerchief-sized apron. She was balancing a tray of empty glasses.

The girl spoke first, "Beany Malone! Only, of course, it isn't Malone now."

"McNally!" Beany breathed, and reached out for her free hand. "I wouldn't have—" She almost said, "I wouldn't have known you." She hurried on, "I tried to phone you when I heard Kay was coming to town. And then—you remember Peggy on our swim team? —she said she tried to reach you for a reunion dance up at Gilfallon Park."

McNally made no allusion to the unanswered phone calls, but asked, "Is this your boy?"

"No, Kay Maffley's. Remember she married Joe Collins? This is their Jodey. You know his dad, don't you? We're looking for him."

"My dad is bigger'n anybody," said Jodey's voice at Beany's side.

Linda McNally looked down at him, and answered as though this was quite a natural remark for a boy to make, "Yes, and I'll bet he can lick anybody, too. Joe hasn't stopped in yet, Beany. Sit here at this table where you can watch the door."

She indicated a chair for Jodey, and said as though it were also a quite natural thing for a little boy to bring a vase of violets to the Buckeye Bar and Grill, "They'll look nice on the table, Jodey." (Beany, looking at cars and people, hadn't noticed he was still holding tight to his bouquet.)

"I picked them myself," he told McNally.

"I thought you did because they have such nice long stems. You'd like a drink, wouldn't you? See that container there by the juke box? Go over and pick out one, and then I'll show you how to open it." She made no fuss over him but treated him as an equal. And Jodey responded to it by going over to where bottles and cracked ice nestled together.

"Joe told me Kay is in the hospital," McNally said. "She hasn't had a turn for the worse, has she?"

"No, it isn't that." Beany quickly summed up the situation of the grandfather who thought a good blistering would solve all Jodey's behavior problems. "Kay's worried sick about it. Jodey's pretty mixed up as it is—"

"He's afraid," McNally said gently. They both glanced toward the soft-drink container and the small figure who was glaring in tight-lipped enmity at a woman who, in passing, said, "Whose nice little boy are you?" in the custardy voice so many put on for a child.

McNally walked over to him and the bottle of his choice, and showed him how to hold it beneath the opener and give it a wrench. She stuck two straws in it for him. She brought a drink to Beany before she went on swift feet to pick up an order off the bar and serve it. Beany watched her capably handling the steady stream of customers at the Buckeye.

Whatever happened to McNally who laughed all over?

Life seemed to have gone over her with a steam roller that had taken away her near chubbiness, her red cheeks, and the lilt in her voice. If the customers she waited on had ever seen her eyes turn into sparkling slits, they'd know the smile she gave them was just a pinned-on one.

Whatever happened to McNally who got a degree to teach kindergarten? Whatever happened to her campus romance with—the name came vaguely back—*Phil Somebody*—

She looked up to see Joe Collins pushing through the door. In his rumpled Bartell coverall, he looked grimy, weary, hot, and older than his twenty-four years. Beany hurried to meet him. She told him of the phone call he must make to Peachtree and the reason for it.

He was quick to understand and to act. He pulled silver out of his pocket and said as he counted it, "So old Gramps is driving down with Brady, huh? Brady can't get off work till around five—works in the shoe store. Beany, have you got change for a dollar, in case I don't have enough? Well, hi there, buckaroo. Tell McNally to bring me a beer and sandwich while I get on the phone."

"I can open bottles," Jodey bragged.

"Swell. Open my beer for me," he said over his shoulder.

His sandwich and beer waited for quite a while before he came and sat down. "I stopped Grandpa right in his tracks," he said and took a thirsty draft of beer. "A little town has its advantages at times." He paused to attack his sandwich. "When I called our house—Grandpa's—and no one answered, I switched the call next door, and the woman said he had gone to get a haircut for his trip to Denver." He lifted his eyes to the big clock over the bar. "I barely caught him at the barbershop in time."

"Is Grandpa coming to take me home with him?" Jodey asked.

"He is *not*. How could Beany and I get along without you?" He picked his words a little more carefully for Beany. "It was like fireworks exploding in my ear. But I told him he would only waste his time and his share of the gas by coming." He took the final swallow of beer from his glass.

Jodey said, "I can open another bottle for you."

But his father got stiffly to his feet. "I haven't got time, son. It's a long trek out to Oberlin Park where the Young Dems are waiting and champing at the bit." He winked at Beany, "Not that they're craving soft drinks, but what they'll be stirring into them. I won't be able to see Cooky till I get back and shower and change. Maybe you can get word to her, Beany, that Grandpa will be sleeping in his own bed in Peachtree tonight."

When Joe was gone and McNally was back at their table, Beany spoke her thoughts aloud, "Kay was so terribly worked up when she talked to me. I'd give anything to see her and tell her that Joe stopped her grandfather from coming. So she can relax. It's hard to get a message through. You have to get the desk on the second floor and leave a message there to have Mrs. Holden call. Jodey, if I took you, would you wait in the car for just a few—?"

"No. No. I don't want to go to the hospital."

McNally must have heard the something's-going-to-hurt-me in his voice for she said very matter-of-factly, "How'd you like to ride home with me, Jodey, and see where I live? I'm off, just as soon as I turn these checks in. Then Beany can stop by for you on her way home. Okay?"

Jodey considered it, his eyes first on McNally, then on Beany, and then back to McNally. Much to Beany's amazement, he said, "Okay." He thrust the pitcher of violets at Beany. "You take these to Mommie."

9

The door of Room 208 with its No Visitors sign was not ajar this late afternoon but closed tight. Beany rapped softly. She waited for several moments before a harried Mrs. Holden opened it a crack. Seeing Beany, she squeezed herself through the narrow opening and said in a low voice, "She's gotten herself in a terrible state. She can't even keep her medicine down."

"I've got good news for her."

"Oh, thank the good Lord! Go in and tell her. Try to quiet her, Beany. Try to keep her from talking."

Kay was sitting hunched up in bed. *It isn't fair; it isn't fair for sickness to drain the gold out of hair and the blue out of eyes.* Her breathing was labored, and her eyes, sick, anguished, and unduly large in her gray face, turned to Beany.

"Kay, honey, everything is under control. I got hold of Joe, and he phoned Peachtree right away. He caught Grandpa Jethro at the barbershop and told him not to come. So he isn't coming at all."

Kay's thin hands clutched Beany's. "Are—you— sure—he—isn't coming?"

85

Mrs. Holden said, "Lie down, child—lie down now. There's nothing to worry about. Is there, Beany?"

"Not a thing in the world, Kay. Joe said to tell you Grandpa will sleep in his own bed in Peachtree tonight."

Kay collapsed on the pillow, but her voice gasped on, "He isn't a villain, you know. None of them are villains—up there in Peachtree. They all thought they were doing the best thing for Jodey—in pounding the daylights out of him—and tying him to the clothesline. Somebody ought to write a column—even a book—about people that mean so well—and do so ill."

"Look, sweetie, the violets," Beany urged. "Jodey picked them for you. And he was so careful to get a long stem on each one."

The tinkle of bracelet was Mrs. Holden's picking up Kay's left hand and putting her fingers on her pulse. Kay's voice wavered on, "I've tried so hard to get well as fast as I could so I could take Jodey. Even when the medicine made me deathly sick and I'd heave it up, I'd take it again. Didn't I, Eudora?"

"Hush now," the nurse soothed, and Beany said again, "You didn't even look at Jodey's violets." But Kay couldn't hush. "I did everything everybody told me to. I chewed up that damn steak and swallowed it. I let everybody stick needles in me. And now the doctor won't even answer me when I ask him when I can get out so I can take Jodey to the farm—" Sobs lumped her voice. "He just stands there—smelling like aftershave lotion—at the foot—of the bed—and won't answer—"

The nurse put the hand she was holding back in

place. She turned to Beany to say in a low voice, "You stay with her. Try and quiet her while I run out for a minute."

Beany smoothed the bedding over her shoulders— *oh, dear heaven, their thinness!* "You'd never guess who I ran into at the Buckeye Bar and Grill, Kay."

"Grandpa said Jodey had worn his welcome out with you folks."

"A lot Grandpa knows about it. You remember McNally, Kay, and how the three of us cooked together?"

"McNally in her red plaid skirt. . . . I used to stand by Jodey's bed when he was asleep and pray, 'Come out of the dark, Jodey—come into the light—' "

"And Jodey took quite a shine to McNally."

Mrs. Holden was suddenly beside the bed, holding out a capsule to Kay and pouring her a glass of water. "I'll just throw it up," Kay demurred.

"No, not now. You were all upset before." But the nurse moved swiftly from the bed, and came back with a wet washcloth to hold to Kay's forehead.

Kay looked into the dark face bent above her. "Are you *sure* Grandpa isn't coming to get Jodey?"

"Beany said he wasn't coming," the nurse reminded her scoldingly. "She said you didn't have a thing to worry about. You know you can trust Beany."

A flickering smile lit up the drained face. "My old dependable Beany." She seemed to have forgotten that Beany was there beside her. "I would never have got through cooking—I was so dumb—but for her because—"

"Hush now and rest," Mrs. Holden said.

But the thready voice went on, "Beany was always there whenever I needed—whenever I— You see, Fay wasn't a mother. And now—isn't it funny?—she doesn't want anyone to know she's a grandmother."

"She wouldn't!" Beany said with feeling.

Kay was fumbling under the bed covering. "I can't find my bracelet."

Mrs. Holden found it for her and slid it back onto the thin wrist. "It just fell off again, doll. Here it is."

Kay gave a wispy giggle. "It slid off in bed the other day—" Beany had to bend low to hear her. "—and I lay on it—one little football—I think it was a football —pressed into me—and it was like a brand, wasn't it, Eudora? I forgot to tell Joe—"

"You can tell him when he comes tonight," the nurse soothed. "Go to sleep now."

Beany stood on one side of the bed, the nurse on the other, with Kay's jagged breathing between them. Mrs. Holden kept glancing anxiously toward the door.

It was pushed open wide, and through it two attendants wheeled an oxygen tent. Mrs. Holden answered Beany's startled look. "The doctor said she'd rest better under it."

Perhaps it was routine procedure, Beany comforted herself, for Kay said in a barely audible whisper, "I guess I talked myself out of air again. But there's something else—I can't remember—it was about Jodey—" Her eyes were again tortured, entreating.

The oxygen tent was being set up. Beany had time only to squeeze her hand, to assure her, "You're not to worry about him. Remember, Kay honey, I'll take care of Jodey. Remember now."

Kay's eyes thanked her.

Beany had to step aside then. She waited in the hall outside, hoping Mrs. Holden would come out so that she might question her as to whether the oxygen tent was because of Kay's heart. But evidently all the nurse's attention was given to her patient.

Beany made her way down the stairs and out of the hospital. She climbed into the car behind the wheel before she broke down. The guard glanced her way as he checked meters, and then went on. Some nurses going off duty ceased their chatter but briefly as they passed. No doubt, crying was a common sight in the near vicinity of St. Michael's.

The McNally home on Hawthorne Street was in an older part of the city called Capitol Hill, which had once housed Denver's wealthy and notable, but no longer. Now in front of the solid two- and three-story houses of brick or stone, with their wide front porches, bay windows, and a certain turn-of-the-century shabby charm, were signs of rooms for rent. In the paper, the advertisements for these rentals were always preceded by, "Within walking distance of downtown."

Beany stopped in front of a spacious old red sandstone. Its lawn, too, bore the sign, "Room for Rent." Beany walked up the wide steps and across the porch, remembering coming here to parties in high-school days. But even if she had never been inside, she could have predicted just how such an old house was laid out and what its furnishings would consist of.

She pressed the bell and heard McNally's voice somewhere in the depths call, "Come on in, Beany."

Yes, there was the wide center hall with the curving staircase leading upward. There was the statue—wasn't it Winged Mercury?—on the newel post holding a lamp. On one side of the hall was a library; on the other, a parlor; behind it would be the dining room with a built-in sideboard. She could even predict that the dining table would be set squarely in the middle of a dark, well-worn Oriental rug and that under it, convenient to the foot of the lady of the house, there would be a bell to press, which, in the old days, would bring in a maid.

Beany followed the strong brown smell of coffee, fresh paint, and the whirr of a vacuum through the parlor and into the dining room.

Jodey was industriously pushing an old-fashioned vacuum cleaner over the rug. (It *was* a worn and faded Oriental, but the table, instead of sitting in the middle of it, was pushed far to one side.) On a layer of newspapers, McNally was stirring a bucket of very bright yellow paint. There was also a coffee percolator.

McNally poured them both coffee. "Or do you like it flavored with paint smell?" she asked.

"My favorite coffee flavor," Beany said loudly over the hum of the vacuum.

McNally suggested, "If you're not tired, Jodey, you can vacuum the rug in the hall."

He wasn't tired, he said, and transferred himself and the vacuum cleaner there.

Beany told of her visit to the hospital. McNally seemed able to say a great deal in a few words. When Beany said, "Kay worries so terribly about Jodey," she said only, "Yes, of course." Beany told her of Kay's blaming his stay in the Peachtree hospital for the unhappy change in him, and again she nodded in understanding. *"Something* put a deep-seated fear in him."

She poured a little white paint into the bucket of yellow. "I want it bright without being yellow-cab yellow. I plan on painting late tonight, because tomorrow I go on the four-to-midnight shift."

Silence fell, and lengthened. How could one ask, "What about your parents and the car accident I read about?"

McNally answered the unspoken question. "This is for Dad's library, turned bedroom. It needs brightening. We had to have a downstairs bedroom, and we made the pantry into a bath, when Mother was sick for so long. But I'm glad I could take care of her here. Dad lived three weeks after the accident, and it just seemed as though he was always being wheeled in and out of operating rooms."

"Oh, McNally, I'm so ashamed. I read about the accident, but it was about the time Carl's father suddenly died. Carl took it pretty hard, and on top of that, we couldn't find a formula that agreed with Mary Liz. But none of that is any excuse. I meant to call you or come to see you. Me and my paving hell with good intentions."

"That's all right, Beany. There wasn't anything anyone could do."

"And you're all alone? This house is so big—I mean, wouldn't you be better off in something smaller?"

"Yes, it's a lot of house. It's a white elephant—or a reddish one—and mortgaged for as much as it's worth. But these big old houses are a drug on the market, so as long as I can't sell it, I'm renting rooms. I don't suppose you noticed the gray-haired cashier at the Buckeye —Alice Henderson. She has a room here. Her folks came from the same mining town my father's did. She came for Dad's funeral and just stayed on. She has more of a head for business than I have."

There were still those other unanswered questions in Beany's mind. Why aren't you teaching kindergarten instead of waiting on tables at the Buckeye Bar and Grill? And what about your Phil Somebody you were always with on the campus, and his fraternity pin on the red slipovers you wore in those days when your cheeks were just as red?

McNally stirred a little more white into the bright yellow. More silence.

Beany *had* to say it. "When I saw Peggy at Gilfallon Park, she thought maybe you were teaching at the Maria Godwin School. And I said I thought you'd be married by now."

"So did I—once." McNally picked up a rag to rub the paint splash off her fingers. She walked about the room, wiping them, and it was somehow as though she were wringing her hands. She said in a driven voice, "I'll tell you about my blighted romance, and then please, Beany, don't let's have any rehashing of it— ever. Phil and I lived for the day when we'd get our degrees and could be married—"

She stopped short. "What am I saying? It turns out that *I* was the one who lived for the day."

Oh, please, McNally. That downtwisted sneer doesn't belong on you.

McNally began folding the stained paint rag as carefully as though it were a fine linen napkin and, without taking her eyes from it, went on in a too casual voice, "Phil got an engineering job in New Mexico, and I got a teaching job—primary—in the same little town. We were to be married last August and set off right away. Then the car accident happened in July. We postponed the wedding, of course, and Phil went on to his job. He didn't come back for Dad's funeral—he said he had to be out in the field. Mother was pretty bad—her mind went first. I phoned Phil on Thanksgiving Day—just to talk to him." She took a moment to smooth the paint rag she had folded so painstakingly. "His wife answered the phone."

"McNally, I can't believe it. What did you say—or she—or did you talk to Phil?"

"I guess the new wife thought I was one of his cousins here, because she began making excuses about Phil not wanting to come home for Thanksgiving because it was their first one together. On that, I hung up."

"Didn't you even hear from *him*? Surely he couldn't be so scurvy."

McNally's voice was more glib—and more harsh. "No, I didn't even get a Dear Mary letter. And I didn't bundle up the skates or the books or—or the fraternity pin—and send them to him. That's it. Let's not make it a conversation piece."

It was Beany who was close to tears. "I keep thinking about the three of us—you and Kay and me—in cooking and swimming and gym. What did we ever find to laugh about?"

Jodey came back to the room, trundling the vacuum cleaner. Beany said thickly, "We'd better go now, honey."

Again he surprised her by saying, "I can come back and clean your rugs again, McNally."

"*Miss* McNally," Beany corrected automatically.

"I'd like to have you, Jodey," she said.

McNally went to the door with her visitors. She closed it, and leaned against it. *I wish you hadn't walked into the Buckeye today, Beany. So far I've been able to sedatize myself with work—work—work. I don't want anybody raking up those silly, happy days at Harkness. I don't want anybody reminding me of what we—I—planned for my life. I just want to live each day, and not look back or ahead.*

✺ 10 ✺

Beany had no chance to go to St. Michael's until the following Tuesday. But each day Mrs. Holden had reported that Kay was resting easier. And on Monday, when Joe stopped in at Laurel Lane to see Jodey, he, too, told Beany that Cooky looked better than she had for days.

"She had the flowers you sent her, Jodey, right on her lunch tray. They're a little wilted now, but she won't let Eudora throw them out. She keeps saying, 'Jodey picked them for me.' "

"I'll get her some more," he said promptly. "I'll get her a whole, whole lot more."

"And I'll take them over just the first chance I get," Beany promised.

Her artist stepmother often used lengths of neutral green or gray material to cover a wall when she was exhibiting her pictures. And on Tuesday, she brought out the lengthy swathes for Beany to run through her automatic washer.

This was Beany's chance to leave the children while

she went to see Kay. Adair helped Jodey gather not only violets but pansies and a few tiny rosebuds. She inserted a frothy sprig or two of spirea among them and shaped a lacy paper doily around them all to make an old-fashioned nosegay, complete with a bow of purple ribbon.

So with Jodey's fragile and fragrant offering on the seat beside her, Beany drove to St. Michael's. Holding it carefully, she took the stairs rather than the elevator. She paused at the head of the steps for a breath, and glanced toward Room 208, just two doors from where she stood.

Carlton was standing outside the door. He saw her and came swiftly toward her. And in that moment she knew why he was there. She knew by his very trying to appear casual, by the protective way he took her arm, that he had been waiting to intercept her and keep her from walking into Kay's room.

"She's dead," she stated flatly.

He nodded. "Yes. Her heart just suddenly gave out. About an hour ago. They got hold of Joe." He pulled her closer. "I didn't want you—to hear it—alone."

The loss, the pain of it, slowed her heartbeat. Yet she was not surprised. She knew now that she had felt the presence of the dark angel that first day when, holding tight to Jodey, she had stood inside the door and looked at the wan sleeper. She had pretended to Kay, and pretended to herself, that she hadn't.

"How did you know about it, Carl?"

"Joe phoned home to tell you right after you left.

He told Adair, and she called me at the office to tell me you were on the way over. I came out in a cab, so I could drive you home."

And so he could soften the blow for her, she knew. She looked toward Kay's room. "Can't I go in?"

"Better not. Joe is still there, seeing to things and waiting for the doctor. He's holding up pretty well— probably in a state of shock. I'll tend to the business end for him—the hospital expenses, insurance, and such." He steered her down the stairs, his hand both loving and firm on her arm.

It wasn't until they reached the car that Beany realized she was still clutching Jodey's bouquet. She said brokenly, "Carl, look. I can't take it home with me." And yet she couldn't throw it onto the cement walk or driveway to shrivel in the sun and be trampled.

A middle-aged woman was parking her car near theirs. She got out, carrying a gift-wrapped box. Carlton stopped her to ask if she was going to visit a patient in the hospital.

Oh, yes, she said proudly, she was going to see her daughter who had had a new baby boy early this morning. Beany tendered the flowers and asked, "Would you like to take her this bouquet? I brought them to a friend but she's—she's—"

Carlton helped her out, "She's already left."

"Oh, mercy, thank you. Aren't they pretty with that lacy ruffle around them? Susie will love them. And you didn't know your friend had left?"

Beany managed to say, "No. Not until I got here."

Carlton took the driver's seat. He pulled her close and said, "Go ahead and cry on my shoulder. That's why I came."

But she didn't cry. She sat stiff and tense, and said, "How are we going to tell Jodey?"

"Joe is the one to tell him. I asked him out for supper. Wait and let him break it to Jodey." He drove on in silence for awhile and then said, "The funeral will be here in Denver. I thought Joe would have it in Peachtree."

What could one say—dear heaven, what!—to a little boy who asked the minute Beany stepped in the door, "How did Mommie like the flowers with the ribbon on them?" She could only turn her back and pretend to be getting herself a drink so he wouldn't see the sudden gush of tears.

Adair diverted his attention by telling him of a paintbrush she had for him in the car, and took him out to get it.

Beany waited dinner an hour that evening for Joe. She fed and bathed the children and put them to bed. "Can I get up when Dad comes?" his son asked.

"Yes, if you hear him, you can get up, Jodey."

She and Carlton waited another hour before they sat down to a very dried-out meal. Joe hadn't come at eleven.

It was after midnight, and Carlton was saying, "We'd better get some sleep," when they heard a car stop outside, and they both went to the door. It was not Joe's convertible. Carl took in the situation before Beany did, and went hurrying toward the two people who got out of it. One was a man, so unsteady on his feet he was being guided—or rather, propelled—along the flagstone path by a young woman who came only to his shoulder. The man was Joe; the woman, McNally.

Carlton put his shoulder under Joe's limp and swinging arm, and he and McNally maneuvered the big, helpless form through the door, the hallway, and to the living-room couch. McNally was explaining matter-of-factly, as though this were an everyday—or every-night—procedure, "He's been at the Buckeye all evening. We didn't think he'd better drive home in his own car, so one of the fellows helped me load him into mine. Joe told me he had a room on the second floor where he lived. I wasn't sure I could hoist him up the stairs, so I brought him here."

It took all three of them to handle him. He was a belligerent drunk. He had waited at the hospital for old big-shot Kostra to come. Because he had some questions he wanted to ask him. (His slurred words were barely intelligible.) But did old know-it-all show up? No—he couldn't be bothered—

"Just stretch out here, Joe," Carlton said.

No, siree, he wasn't going to stretch out. He was going to run down that old so-and-so and ask him— ask him why he gave Cooky all those newfangled drugs without—without giving one sweet damn what they did to her heart. He was going to track him down—and ram all his fancy gobbledygook down his throat.

Then he turned maudlin, reiterating that he had nothing left to live for. Carlton said, "Beany, make

99

some coffee." She was putting it on when the door of the guest room opened, and there was Jodey going straight to Joe. Joe sobbed out, "She's dead, buckaroo —Cooky is dead," and folded him into his arms.

It wasn't the way Beany would have thought the news should be broken to a disturbed little boy, but maybe it was as good as any. Jodey said nothing; his silence was that of acceptance, as though he already knew or expected it. He wouldn't go back to bed. "I want to stay with Dad."

It ended with their shoving the love seat close to the couch. Joe himself, as Carlton put it, conked out. Carlton pulled off Joe's coat and shoes, and loosened his tie. Beany covered him with an afghan when she covered Jodey with the blanket off his cot. It ended with Carlton, Beany, and McNally sitting in the kitchen and drinking the coffee Beany had made and talking in low, hushed voices. About how some, in their first unbearable grief, drop into a church while some make for a bar. "It's the same instinct," Carlton said.

McNally said nothing about bearing unbearable grief.

❧ II ❧

The morning of Kay's funeral was grayly overcast
with a fine mist in the air. And Beany's heart was even
more overcast as she sat beside Carlton in the small
chapel and waited for the services to begin.

Who would take care of Jodey?

Kay's mother, Fay, the pretty and gushing grandmother who didn't want to be known as a grandmother, had flown in from Hawaii earlier that morning. Joe Collins, edgy and unpredictable since Kay's
death, had refused to meet his mother-in-law's plane.
"Let her pay for a taxi, and have that much less for
Chanel No. 5," he stormed.

Carlton had driven to the airport and met Fay. He
had stopped in Laurel Lane for Beany and then driven
on to the chapel so that Fay could join Joe and the
relatives from Peachtree.

Joe's older sister Aline and her husband had driven
from Peachtree, bringing Grandma Collins and Kay's
Grandpa Jethro and also the youngest of Aline's four,
a placid six-months-old with not enough hair to identify

it as to sex, who was strapped to a padded L-shaped carrier that Beany and her friends called a bundle-board.

Beany and Carlton had shaken hands with them and asked them to stop at their house for a buffet lunch after the service before taking the long drive back to Utah. Joe's sister Aline clutched Beany's arm and drew her a little aside from the other mourners in the front row to say in a folksy whisper, "I guess Joe told you he was coming back to his job in Peachtree. You've certainly been wonderful to him and Kay, but I'll bet you've had your hands full with Jodey. In Peachtree, we had to take him in shifts. He'd wear first one to a frazzle—and then—"

Beany was thankful when the baby sneezed sudsily, and Aline had to hunt for a tissue. Beany and Carlton took their seats in the back of the chapel.

Yes, Joe and Jodey were going back to Peachtree. A telegram had come to Joe yesterday from this same sister:

KEITH SAYS YOUR OLD JOB IS WAITING FOR YOU.

Beany, who had listened to Joe's railing against his cousin, was surprised at how pleased with the offer he seemed. "Do you think you'll go back, Joe?"

"There's nothing to keep me here now. The only thing Denver's got for me is a university, but I'm too bogged down in debt to think about that. I guess Keith isn't as bad as I thought—to be sending me word to come back."

If Jodey hadn't been clinging as close to Joe as his

own shadow, she could have said, "Kay didn't like the way the folks there treated Jodey." Or if Joe hadn't still been so stunned and bewildered with grief, she could have talked it over with him. Yet what could she say? As Carlton reminded her again and again, "Joe is Jodey's father. He's the one to make decisions."

She had accused him, "You don't want me to keep on looking after Jodey—that's it, isn't it, Carl?"

She had to wait for his slow answer, "You've no idea how much the care of him has taken out of you. You get the whole brunt of it."

"But he's been coming out of his shell. Look at how he made up with McNally. Kay told me how the folks in Peachtree lambasted him—and I promised her—"

"Beany, Beany, promises or not, he's Joe's son, not yours."

The chapel was so silent you could hear Aline's baby sucking on its pacifier. The background organ music started and drowned it out just as Beany's father and stepmother came in and sat down across the aisle. Adair wiped tears away as the organ played on; perhaps she was remembering the luminous bride who wanted to paint her happiness into a picture of peach blossoms.

Ander and Mary Fred made the two-hour drive from Wyoming to pay final tribute to Kay. As they moved into seats next to Beany and Carl, Ander looked at the front of the small chapel where Joe and his family sat, and asked, "Jodey isn't here?"

"No, he's home with our two," Beany said. "Mc-

Nally, an old friend of Kay's and mine, offered to stay with them."

"That's better," Ander answered in relief.

Kay's nurse, Mrs. Holden, came in and found a seat by herself apart from the others. It took a second glance for Beany, used as she was to seeing her in white, to recognize her in her brown-checked cotton suit and a hat that rode high on her graying hair, done in a knot.

Beany and Carlton moved over to sit next to her, and Beany asked her to come over to their house for lunch afterward. Mrs. Holden thanked her but explained that she was on a night shift at the hospital and hadn't had any sleep yet.

"I have all of Kay's things at home," she added. "Her husband was so broken up I told him I'd pack everything and take them to you. I can bring them to you tomorrow if that's convenient."

"Yes, Eudora. Come, and please plan to stay for coffee."

There was another person in the scattered handful in the chapel that Beany glanced at through tear-blurred eyes and tried to place. It was a young woman in a navy-blue dress, and white gloves, hat, pumps, and bag. Even her sheathed umbrella was navy with white polka dots. Where had Beany seen that auburn hair and the face beneath it that was almost, but not quite, pretty?

Dulcie and Trig came, too. Beany recognized Trig's dark suit as the one he had been married in and had worn on only a few special occasions. Dulcie stopped to whisper to Beany, "I brought some sliced turkey, like I said, to feed Joe's folks. And some extra cups. They're in the car."

Beany murmured her thanks.

Dulcie, too, looked toward the occupants of the front row close to the flower-covered casket. "Is that all that came from Peachtree—just those four—five—?"

"One carful," Beany whispered.

"So the gilded lily came from Hawaii!"

"Sh-h-h," Beany breathed, for just then Father Andrew Kern—the Andy who had danced with Beany and Kay at Harkness—stepped behind the podium. The organ ceased playing. He asked that angels lead Kay into paradise. *"Requiescat in pace."*

Beany's tears started in eyes already sore from previous tears. The ache under her ribs grew more unbearable— Carlton slid his arm around her.

Who would take care of Jodey?

Fay had left no doubt that she was out of the running. On the drive to the chapel she had wiped away tears with a perfumed handkerchief. "I wish my life was so I could look after Kay's little boy. Such an adorable blond child. Oh, it isn't that I live a butterfly existence—everybody used to call me Fay, the Gay—but now I'm a working girl. I spend several afternoons a week in a curio and gift shop on Maui."

Father Kern was saying the last prayer, "And let perpetual light shine upon her."

It wasn't until Carl and Beany stopped to give Aline and her husband directions for getting to Laurel Lane that Beany identified the girl in the navy blue and the careful white accessories. She, too, had come up to greet the Peachtree relatives, and Grandma Collins exclaimed, "For gracious sake—Vonnie! Look here, Aline and Vern, here's Yvonne Plettner."

So the perfectly turned-out girl was the one-time girl friend of Joe Collins, and present lab technician at St. Michael's. It would have seemed rude not to ask her to join her old neighbors, so Beany invited her to stop off at the Buells' for refreshments.

She'd *just love to,* because the Plettners and the Collinses were *just like kinfolks,* but she had to get back to the hospital. "I hope you'll give me a rain check."

Her gushing didn't ring true to Beany. Nor was there a sign of tears in those light blue eyes.

The mist had changed to a half-hearted drizzle when Beany held open the Buell front door for the Peachtree contingent. "Where's Jodey?" each one asked.

He was nowhere visible. Beany and Carl had been the first to return from the funeral. The three children had been helping McNally set out spoons on the table. But when simultaneously there came the sound of car doors slamming and familiar voices, Jodey had run for cover. Out the French doors, down the length of the yard with Thumper at his heels, and under the damp spirea bushes.

Beany evaded their question with, "He's out in the back yard. Maybe Joe can bring him in later. But sit down and have some hot coffee."

She made introductions of Mary Fred and Ander, Dulcie and Trig, and McNally to the Peachtree folks. Father Kern had already introduced himself at the chapel. Dulcie was taking over the dispensing of the food. She motioned to Beany and told her, "Now when I pass the platter of cold meat, you come along with the hot rolls."

Beany passed them to the short, ruddy, and peppery Grandpa Jethro. (The blisterer of behinds.) He was bald except for a scant fringe of hair that ran from the back of one ear to the back of the other. Beany even marveled that he had been at the Peachtree barbershop long enough for Joe Collins to reach him there and tell him not to come to Denver for Jodey.

He took a roll and said, "You ought to get Jodey in out of the rain. I want to see if he's filled out any."

Again Beany evaded, "The rain has about stopped. He likes to be by himself."

She heard him mutter to his daughter, Fay, "High time somebody got hold of that kid that will make him toe the mark."

Who'll take care of Jodey? Please God, not Grandpa Jethro.

Beany passed the rolls to Kay's mother next. Fay didn't take one because they were buttered. "Me, and my battle with the bulge," she said coyly. Very original, Beany thought viciously, and hated her for looking so radiant, so size-ten, so even younger than her daughter had looked at St. Michael's.

Joe's mother sat on a corner of the couch. She was a tired-eyed, buffeted woman who looked as if she felt slightly aggrieved at life for having dealt with her so harshly. She reached for a roll, and said in a peevish voice, "I don't know why Joe didn't tell us Kay was so sick. We all thought they could build her up in the hospital. Aline and I used to say we didn't think she ate enough."

Beany asked, "Was the trip down pretty tiring?"

"Yes, it was. We drove all night because Aline's husband wanted to get in a day's work yesterday. They kept telling me to sleep, but I can't sleep in a car."

The solidly-built Aline and her untalkative husband sat on the love seat with the baby, now out of the bundle-board, wedged between them. Aline was tugging at the skirt of her black dress, trying to cover her sizable knees. She gave Beany her same folksy smile and said, "It's small for me. I had to borrow it because I didn't have a black dress to my name."

She put two rolls on her husband's plate, and two on her own. "We've got a long ride ahead of us. Vern and I took turns driving on the way down. The baby slept practically the whole time, and the two old folks dozed in the back seat. Of course, according to them, they never closed an eye." She laughed with hearty relish.

She took another roll, broke off the top crust and expertly tucked it into her baby's fist. She looked the Buell house over with bright-eyed interest. "Look Vern, Beany's got a service room there for her washing machine and ironing board. I just love these new one-story houses like this with no basement," she told Beany. "It's so nice—" nodding toward the French doors "—to step right outside into your yard. I see you've got one of those clothesbaskets on wheels. I can't use one because of the steps at our house. Honestly, steps to go up, steps to go down every time I turn around."

But it hadn't kept her thin. She was the the kind who would accrue a few extra pounds each year, and all her activity, instead of taking them off, would only solidify them. *Why,* Beany thought irrelevantly, *do hearty, bustling women so often marry meek and wispy men?*

Who would look after Jodey? Aline wasn't unkind. Surely she would do away with the rope and the clothesline if she understood Jodey's inner problems. Beany planned to have Ander explain them to her and make a plea for more understanding and gentleness and love.

Dulcie and Trig left as soon as the cake was passed. Dulcie nodded toward Joe, who was standing across the room glowering at his own folks. "Looks like a family knockdown and drag-out to me," she said.

Father Kern followed soon. Beany opened the door for him, and he said as he had so often in days gone by, "Stay as sweet as you are, knucks."

McNally was refilling coffee cups when Grandpa Jethro exploded to her, "Can't any of you get that kid in the house where he belongs? Where is he anyway?"

"He's out in the yard under some bushes," McNally said evenly.

"We'll be leaving pretty quick. You'd think he'd want to see his own folks that did for him when his mother wasn't able to."

His daughter, Fay, said, "Now, Daddy, don't work yourself up."

And Joe turned his set face toward his folks and said spitefully, "Maybe the kid knows when he's well off. I wish I had a bush to crawl under. All I've got is criticism from everyone of you. From the minute you landed, all I've heard is chip-chip-chip."

His mother's complaining voice said, "Now, Joe, it's just that everybody in Peachtree thought it was funny you'd have the funeral here instead of bringing Kay home."

"Home!" he flung out. "Peachtree wasn't home to Cooky. If she didn't want any part of it when she was alive, I damn-sure wasn't going to—to—" His voice broke, and he turned and busied himself at the table.

After a pause that seemed uncomfortably long, Joe's sister said in an overly casual manner, "Are you planning on coming back right away, Joe? As long as Keith said—well, I think you ought to get there as soon as you can."

"I've got things to tend to here. I'm not burning up the road just to please old big-britches Keith."

Aline's husband turned his eyes on Joe and half opened his mouth. But he looked at his wife, and evidently decided to leave the talking to her.

She, in her big-sister role, said, "Now, look here, Joe, you had no business flying off the handle with Keith the way you did that time on the phone. But Vern talked to him, and I talked to him, and your father talked to him, and we—well, he said he was willing to make allowances for your being upset over

Kay. But we had to do a lot of fixing things for you, so you just better not start throwing your weight around again."

"Well, I'll be a horn toad!" Joe said in slow wonder. "So all you folks had to go licking his boots to get him to give me my job back. And now I'm to go back, dragging my tail. Oh, no! No, thank you, ma'am. I've got a job here and—"

Again a sputtering explosion from Grandpa Jethro, "Don't talk like a fool. You've got a job here! Yes, and you've got a boy, too, that somebody has to look after."

"I can look after my own kid," Joe said.

Undaunted, the old man roared back, "You'll look after him! How? How when you're driving a truck from morning till evening? You can't hire anybody to look after a kid as out of kilter as he is. You can't keep imposing on these friends of Kay's. I'd say they have about all they can handle. Before you get so high and mighty, just remember that blood is thicker than water."

Joe had no answer. Perhaps he was remembering his landlady with whom Jodey had not even lasted three days.

Aline had evidently decided that now, with Joe's belligerence shriveled to nothing, was the time to put in her oar. "Grandpa Jethro is right about Jodey being out of kilter, Joe," she said firmly. "Now don't get me wrong—nobody blames Kay. He was just too much for her. So you come back to your job, and I'll look after Jodey. Only I can't be pampering him and making it harder on me and my family. I don't hold with all those excuses Kay made for him—about his tantrums and his running away being from some psychological— oh, damage or fear or whatever."

Grandma Collins showed her agreement by weary nods of the head, and Grandpa Jethro by vociferous ones. He pointed to Mary Liz, asleep on her aunt's lap, and Mister, offering a cube of sugar to Aline's baby. "See those two! They've been taught to behave."

Aline ended her speech sententiously, "You don't do any kid a favor by spoiling him rotten. You only make it tougher for him later on, because the world has to hammer it out of him."

Beany's heart had dropped to the soles of her feet. No argument or plea from Ander could ever penetrate such hide-bound convictions. She looked imploringly at Carlton who, with Ander, stood in the dining end of the room.

Carlton stepped out from behind the table and said, "Just a minute, folks." In the few years he had been practicing law, he had acquired that certain authority which made people listen to him. "You're right, all of you. Jodey and his needs are what Joe must consider now. Maybe his going back to Peachtree would mean another uprooting for Jodey. Maybe Joe's staying on here would be the better choice. And Grandpa Jethro, Beany doesn't feel Jodey is an imposition. She'd be unhappy if he left. Right, Beany?"

"That's right," she choked out. Carlton flashed her a look that said: *I know looking after Jodey will take a lot out of you, but I couldn't take any more of their drawing and quartering him.* And she looked back with her heart in her eyes: *Carl, I adore you. I'll never over-cook your three-minute egg again. I worship you.*

No one argued or disputed with him, or with Joe when he said briefly, "I'm staying."

It wasn't until the Peachtree car had left and Carlton had driven off to the airport with Fay that Joe slipped into the backyard and called, "Come on now, buckaroo, the folks are gone," and Jodey wormed his damp, blue-lipped self out from his hideaway with a hailing of white flowerlets on his yellow head.

Mary Fred carried in the dead weight of her niece and deposited her in her crib. She said several times to Ander, "We ought to be going." But his gray, thoughtful eyes followed Jodey. Joe had changed him into dry clothes, and Beany made him hot chocolate to drink with his roll sandwich. Ander tried to talk to him but he, clinging close to his father, would only say, "My dad's bigger'n you."

Again as the station wagon headed north to Wyoming, it was Mary Fred who did the talking and Ander who kept his eyes on the road, dark and glistening with rain, and answered only in grunts or monosyllables. They were well out on the plains by the time Mary Fred, in her postmorteming all that had happened, wound up with, "That Fay! She could even cry and look glamorous. And poor Beany with her eyes like stewed rhubarb."

This time he didn't answer at all. Again she touched his arm and said, "Come back, come back, wherever you are." He didn't seem to hear her, and she tugged more demandingly with something like fear in her eyes, "Or at least take me with you."

He smiled at her, a rather aloof and polite smile. "How old was Jodey when Joe and Kay moved back to Peachtree with him?"

"Let's see—they went back in May or June, and he was born the September before. About nine or ten months. He was just beginning to walk."

"Do you remember if he crawled before he walked?"

She knew why he was asking. Brain-damaged or re-tarded children seldom progressed in the chronological pattern. "Yes, I sure do. I can see him yet. Whenever one of us would go to see Kay and the baby up over the garage, our red setter would go with us. Little Jodey was crazy about him, and he'd crawl after him lickety-cut."

"And he wasn't afraid of people? Or of going to sleep in the dark?"

"Heavens, no. He'd reach out his arms to anyone. And sometimes Beany would baby-sit for him. She'd bring him over to our house, and put him in one of the rooms and turn out the light and shut the door."

"Something has pushed him under a dark cloud. I wish I hadn't had to get back to take care of the out-patients. I'd have liked to talk more to Joe and Beany about the poor kid."

⚛ 12 ⚛

The next afternoon Beany opened the door in welcome to Eudora Holden, who came up the flagstone path carrying Kay's suitcase, a garment box, and the green, boat-shaped vase that had held the flowers telegraphed from Hawaii.

The suitcase Beany put in the storage closet. Later on either she or Joe could decide about its contents. She would give Mrs. Kincaid the green barge for her flower arrangements. The very sight of it stirred Beany's unchristian malice toward the woman who had picked up the phone and ordered it when a letter would have meant far more to her daughter.

Eudora opened the garment box. "I took her gowns and bed jacket home and washed and ironed them. And I put in all the gifts that you folks and her friends sent."

There they were, the filmy gowns Beany had brought home and laundered and taken back, so Kay needn't wear hospital ones. There was the bright, splashy bed jacket Dulcie had stitched up for her. Her mad, mod poncho, Kay had called it. There were the powders and colognes and lotions—and the fuzzy slippers Joe had shopped for. Kay had never walked in them.

Beany put the lid back on the box. "You said once that you had a young married daughter, Eudora. Take these things to her, because—"

"I know." She helped Beany retie the string and added simply, "Thank you, Beany."

"What about the bracelet, Eudora? Is it in the suitcase?"

Mrs. Holden gave her a swift, uneasy look. "That's another reason I wanted to come today. To tell you about it. There's a lab technician at St. Michael's who knew Kay and her husband—"

"Yes, I met her—Yvonne Plettner."

"That's right. She used to run in now and then to see how Kay was doing and to talk to Joe. She came in that last morning when Kay was in a coma, and I was working over her. I had put the bracelet on the bedside table. I heard it clink, and then I noticed it in the pocket of that girl's nylon smock. Maybe she gave it to Joe."

Beany shook her head. "She didn't. He asked me about it last evening." She told herself there was no reason for her to be so upset because Kay's bracelet was in Yvonne's keeping. But she said, "I'd just feel better if either Joe or Jodey had it."

Perhaps the nurse felt the same way, for she said, "I inquired at the office. Yvonne is off at four today, and I got her address. It's not far from here. She should be home by now. If you want to go, I'll stay here with the little ones."

Beany lost no time in getting into the car and setting out for Yvonne's address. It was a new, white-brick apartment house called, coincidentally enough, "The Yvonne." Beany could imagine Yvonne saying in her pert way, "They named the apartment house after me." Its twin next to it was called "The Margot."

In the vestibule, Beany saw that Yvonne Plettner and a Marcia Stone occupied apartment number 27. She pressed the button and heard the buzz that meant the latch was off the inner door. She went in, climbed the carpeted stairs, and rapped on the door of number 27.

It was opened not by Yvonne but by a girl using a huge bath towel as cover, and who let out a startled scream as she backed up and said, "For Pete's sake, I was sure it was Vonnie—that she forgot her key—"

"I came to see Yvonne."

"She'll be home any minute. She must have stopped at the store. But come on in. I'm Marcie."

"I'm Beany Buell."

"Are you one of her friends from Utah?"

"No. But I'm a friend of a girl that came from Peachtree. She introduced me to Yvonne at the hospital."

"Oh, you mean Kay, the one that died and whose funeral Vonnie went to yesterday?"

How casually an outsider could speak of death when it didn't concern him. "Yes, Kay," Beany said. "We've been friends ever since we were in high school."

"Oh, that's too bad. But then I guess the poor little thing had been sickly for so long, and never could have got well. I guess she'd just been a millstone on her husband's neck ever since they were married, and like they say, sometimes death is a blessing in disguise."

Beany looked at the girl's bland face, and felt anger slowing her heartbeat. She said, "I'm sure you're only quoting what you've heard someone else say—about Kay being a millstone. Because if you knew her, or her husband, you'd never make such a—"

"Oh, I'm sorry." Marcia clutched the towel tighter around her and backed farther away, stammering, "I never meant—I mean, maybe I'm thinking of someone else." She backed on until she was out of the room, saying as she went, "I've got to tear into my clothes. I'm on the split shift at the phone company."

Beany's anger was still with her when Marcia went hurrying off and when Yvonne came in a few minutes later. Again Yvonne looked very perfectly turned out —a flowered print today and matching green pumps.

She greeted Beany cordially, "It's nice to see you again. Have you been waiting long?"

Long enough to hear your roommate quote you on Kay's being a millstone around Joe's neck. "No, not long. I just ran over to get Kay Collins's bracelet."

Her bluntness seemed to catch Yvonne off guard. "Bracelet?" she said in a startled voice. "Why, what makes you think I have Kay's bracelet?"

"Her nurse, Eudora Holden, told me you came in to see Kay that last morning, and that you picked it up and—"

"Well, am I ever stupid! I didn't know what you meant for a minute. At Peachtree we never called them a bracelet. We always called them the ball and chain, because they were just that. When a fellow put the little trophies he'd earned on a chain and gave it to a girl, it meant she wasn't free to date anyone else. It was the same as an engagement ring, or a frat pin—and that's why we called them—"

"I know. Kay told me." To save herself, Beany couldn't be anything but cold and standoffish.

"I'll get it for you," Yvonne said.

She came back and handed Beany a small, square box. She was talking even more glibly. "I guess you don't know how hospitals are. Honestly, you can't lay down a thermometer or a ballpoint without its disappearing. So when I ran in to Kay's room that last morning, I could tell she was bad, and I saw the ball and chain where it had dropped on the floor. I didn't want anything to happen to it, so I picked it up and just instinctively dropped it in my pocket."

Beany made herself murmur that it was nice of her.

And then perhaps Yvonne wanted to pay back the one who had told Beany of her taking the bracelet, for she added, "Some of the special nurses are honest as the day is long, but we've all learned that our colored brethren—and that means sisters, too—are pretty darn sticky-fingered."

Beany longed to tell her that she, Yvonne, had been the sticky-fingered one in this case. But Carlton always reminded her, "Telling off people is a luxury few can afford." So she only said as she took the box with its clinking contents, "Thank you, Yvonne. Kay always wanted Jodey to have it."

"I'd have given anything to visit with all the folks that came down for the funeral yesterday. Only I didn't have time. We used to live next door to the Collinses. My dad—he owns the Plettner garage and filling station and the Ford dealership—gave Joe his first job." A pause, and then the close friend of the Collins family asked, "Did Joe take Kay's death pretty hard?"

"Yes, he did. He loved her so." *I dare you to say anything about Kay being a millstone around his neck.*

"What about Joe? Is he going back to Peachtree?"

"No, he'll stay on at his job at Bartell's."

"Oh. What about Jodey? Which one decided to take him? Or did all the folks from Peachtree let him decide?"

Not for worlds would Beany have admitted to the girl who had said that Jodey was the worst little monster ever to come to the Peachtree hospital that he had taken cover under the wet spirea bushes all the time his relatives were there. "Jodey did his deciding for Joe. He's staying on with us so he can see more of him."

"Is Joe living with you?"

"No, he has a room where he doesn't have so far to drive to work." Did she imagine that Yvonne found that bit of information pleasing? "But he keeps in close touch with Jodey." Beany took a step toward the door.

"Oh, don't rush off. I can fix coffee in a jiff. And

look, I've got fresh cupcakes." The apartment was so small, she had only to take a few steps to reach the kitchen and hold up a plate of cupcakes with the pinkest pink frosting—and made even deeper by tiny lumps of purplish red—that Beany had ever laid eyes on. Yvonne added, "Whenever I'm upset, I bustle around and cook up something. That's strawberry icing. You can make it out of fresh berries; only I used jam for these."

Beany was glad she had the excuse of the children at home for not staying on. She was in no mood for more of Yvonne's prying about Joe Collins and his small son.

At home, she found Mister and Mary Liz carrying on a conversation with Eudora Holden. Jodey lingered on the outer fringe.

Beany had planned for Joe to give his son the bracelet with his own athletic trophies. But Jodey seemed to have sensitive antennae, like an insect, that told him what was in the air. She was no sooner in the house than he asked, "Did you get the bracelet with all the footballs and baseballs on it? Can I have it now?"

"Yes. You can show it to everyone, and you can look at it yourself. But you must never take it outside. Okay?"

A little boy of surprises. Pridefully he showed the bracelet to Mary Liz and Mister and Mrs. Holden. He sat down on the couch, tolling over the engraved balls like a religious with a rosary, and fell asleep while doing so.

Beany and her guest had coffee and some of the ice cream and cake left over from yesterday's lunch. They talked in low tones. "There's one thing I wanted to ask you, Eudora. Was Kay's death brought on by her getting so worked up about her grandfather coming for Jodey? Or was she—was she so bad when she went into the hospital?"

Mrs. Holden spooned some of the hot coffee over her ice cream, and said, "I've had some dental work done, and I can't stand anything real hot or real cold yet. Do you mean was little Kay already doomed when she came to St. Michael's?" Her face settled into graver lines. "I think so, Beany, I think so. You might say she was doomed even before that. Even before she had a miscarriage because she was so anemic. Even before her fainting spells started when she was carrying Jodey. Yes, maybe from the time she was a child, and had no one to see that she built up health and strength. She was all heart and spirit. You see, I know a lot about her. She talked to me so much. I'd sit beside her bed at night and hold her hand—"

"I didn't know you were with her at night, Eudora. I thought you were just on days."

"I was her only private nurse. I was there from eight in the morning till four in the afternoon. But on her bad days, I'd rest awhile in the nurse's lounge and go back until she quieted down for the night. They always emphasize in training that a nurse should never let her emotions get involved with a patient. I don't often, but I couldn't help it with Kay." It took her awhile to steady her lips before she added, "She thought so much of you, Beany."

Beany dabbed at her tears with a paper napkin.

The woman's gentle voice went on, "I know how grieved you are over this. But I want to tell you something, child. I have seen a lot of death—as a person and as a nurse. I've seen a lot of grief in the ones that were bereaved. And your grief for Kay, and her husband's grief for her, is what I call a clean wound. Before you know it, you'll be able to smile and say, 'I remember how Kay used to do—or say—' It's when there's bitterness or regret or guilt that the wound festers on and on, and never really heals."

Beany could only choke out, "I suppose so."

"And then," the nurse mused on as she got to her feet and began drawing on her gloves, "there's one thing that seems to me worse than grief. And that's when there's death, and the ones who are left feel no grief and have no tears to shed. That is the saddest of all."

They both stood looking down at the tousled blond head on the couch. Beany gathered Mary Liz into her arms to keep her quiet, and she and the nurse talked on in even lower voices about Jodey and his problems.

"What do you think will help him, Eudora?"

"All the love you can give him, Beany. They used to believe that certain people were possessed of devils. They were—and they still are, and the devils still have to be cast out. This little boy's devils are fear and mistrust and insecurity."

Beany opened the door for her, and kissed her good-bye.

"I'm so glad Kay had *you*," she said.

It didn't make sense, but Beany and Carlton quarreled bitterly the next morning over none other than Yvonne Plettner.

Beany had had no chance the night before to tell him about Yvonne and the bracelet because of his absorption in legal papers. Breakfast was not the best time in the world to carry on a conversation, what with Mister insisting that he could pour his own milk (and he could, but he didn't always stop pouring in time); and having to keep plopping Mary Liz back down in her high chair (by standing up and bending over she could reach more on the table); and by saying to Jodey, "Eat your egg before it gets cold." (He was inclined to sit and stare into space.)

But Beany related the whole story from the time the bracelet lay on the hospital bedside table until she herself put it into Jodey's hands. "You can't tell me that our two-faced little Miss Yvonne didn't plan to latch on to it herself." She had put some halved biscuits into the toaster. They were smaller than a slice of bread, so that instead of their popping up high enough to pull out, she had to reach in for them. She burned a finger in the process.

Carlton said, "Do you always go around accusing a person of stealing when you haven't the slightest—"

Beany took the burned finger out of her mouth, and mocked, "—not the slightest basis of fact? Basis of fact, or not, I wouldn't trust her as far as I could throw a cat. I think she figured she had a right to the bracelet because Joe went with her before—"

"You think! Your thinking isn't thinking. It's pure prejudice. Do you know that just such senseless jumping to conclusions can lead to a slander suit?"

The burned finger hurt, and so did her husband's cold logic. She flung out, "Oh, for Pat's sake. Don't be so pontifical. You're around Uncle Matthew so much, you sound just like him."

Carlton was silent. But his very getting up to refill his coffee cup, his ignoring her as though her remark wasn't worth answering, made her go further. "I used to blame Uncle Matthew's wife for always going off to visit one of the girls and staying on and on. Heavens, no wonder! Poor Aunt Ruth probably never opened her mouth that he didn't tell her she was talking like a fool because she didn't have legal proof for every word she said."

At that very moment the person under discussion knocked on the door and came in. "Just half a cup of coffee, my dear," Uncle Matthew told Beany. "Carl and I have to meet with the beneficiaries of that Cullen estate early this morning."

A third party entering in the midst of a quarrel is like putting the unsolved resentments in deep freeze. Carlton left without kissing her good-bye. Beany sat on at the breakfast table with no heart for the work that clamored to be done. She looked sourly at the rumpled rugs on the living-room floor. A lot of good it would do to shake them and lay them flat. The next time she looked they would only be wadded up again.

An hour went by, and she could stand it no longer. She dialed the Buell law office and asked for Carl. The secretary said, "Beany, could he call you back? He's tied up right now."

"Ring him anyway, Connie. What I have to say won't take a sec."

The minute Beany heard his "Carlton Buell speaking," she tumbled out, "I had to call you. I was just too heartsick even to hunt up the dirty laundry. I didn't mean a single word of it. I wouldn't blame *you* for suing me for slander. I'm just an old shrew."

She heard the pause at his end, and suddenly remembered the beneficiaries' meeting. He was probably sitting at the table with Uncle Matthew and the parties involved.

He answered, choosing his words because of his listeners, "I don't agree with that last statement at all. And—and neither do I think there's any cause for suit. Thank you for calling—I was hoping I'd hear from you this morning, Mrs.—" He hesitated, groping for a name and then said, "Mrs. Cutty."

It was his "Mrs. Cutty"—he hadn't dared say Cutty Sark—that set her to giggling and wiping tears away as she gathered up clothes for the washer.

❧ 13 ❧

The hot, exhausting, trying days of June!

So few people understood Jodey. So few realized that the same dark fears that made him scream out in terror at night made him act like a belligerent brat by day.

The husband of the couple who lived to the north of the Buells' was away in army service. The wife traveled for a cosmetic firm. On one of the rare occasions when she was home and in an even rarer spirit of neighborliness, she came to the fence with three small dolls for the children. Beany judged by their scent that they had been used in a perfume display.

Both Mister and Mary Liz accepted theirs happily and, after a nudge from their mother, thanked the donor. Jodey wouldn't even come close to the fence. He backed away, saying emphatically, "No. No. I don't want it."

Even as Beany tried to explain that he was fearful of strangers, the young and competent woman said coldly, "It's amazing how few children are taught manners these days," and stalked away.

Beany leaned against their small cherry tree and prayed: *Give me of your strength—and wisdom.*

Another time when a trip to the supermarket was a must, she took the three children with her. Mary Liz would always ride happily in the grocery cart while Mister trotted about helpfully—"I know where the crackers are." But this day when Jodey saw people trickling in and out the doors, he refused to get out of the car. "I don't want to go. I want to stay out here by myself."

"All right, Jodey. We won't be but a few minutes."

Beany came hurrying back in ten to find a stout, middle-aged woman, flushed and irate, standing by the car, holding tight to Jodey. The woman's ire was for Beany. The very idea of leaving a child in a car in the hot sun! *She* had stopped to offer him a candy lozenge, but the poor little thing evidently wasn't used to *kindness* because he had opened the door and tried to run.

"It's plain as the nose on your face that he's been mistreated." She ended with thin-lipped meaning, "Is he your *step*son?"

It was too long a story to tell a woman who had already formed her own opinions. Beany only murmured that Jodey was afraid of people, loaded in children and groceries, and drove off.

She could take her own two children to church, to the library, or to watch Carlton's Bombshells play in the Young America League. But crowds and noise frightened Jodey. He turned into a quivering little rabbit looking for and longing for a hole to hide in.

The one place where he went happily was to the

McNally house. He had learned to dial McNally's number. "Do you want me to clean your carpets?" he would ask.

Why, yes, she would answer, she was just wishing someone could vacuum them. Either she would come to Laurel Lane after him, and have coffee with Beany on the patio, or Beany would drive Jodey, along with Mister and Mary Liz, over to the old red sandstone on Hawthorne, where the coffee percolator still shared the dining table with paint buckets, sandpaper, and patching plaster.

Mister, on his first trip, looked with awe at the many high-ceilinged rooms, hallways, and front and back stairs. "Is this a one-body's house?" he asked.

Jodey, in his superior wisdom, enlightened him, "No, it's a lots-of-body's house. We have roomers."

And diligently, contentedly, he plied the noisy old vacuum.

"You won't have any rugs left, McNally," Beany said.

"That's all right. I've looked at those tired old things too long as it is. It does something for Jodey to feel he can do things. The old human craving to be needed, I suppose."

It was this very wanting to *do* things that caused constant friction between him and Mister. Jodey wanted to be the official opener of soft drinks. So did Mister. They always squabbled over who should hold the dustpan for Beany. When the back yard needed watering, she had to set the timer and give Jodey five minutes of holding the hose, and Mister five. She often let the lawn go unwatered rather than endure the bickering.

Another constant contention between the two was Kay's bracelet. Mister was also entranced by the miniature footballs, baseballs, and basketballs. But Jodey cherished it jealously.

Before he became a member of the Buell household, baby-sitters had never been a problem for Beany. Even though Adair gave much time to her painting, and Mrs. Kincaid, next door, to her day nursery work, they often volunteered. But Jodey was uneasy with them. The schoolgirls Beany could call on were at a complete loss in handling him. So was the mother of the three little boys across the street who had always traded baby-sitting with Beany. "That kid stumps me," she admitted.

In desperation Beany had to accept the services of Dotty's sixteen-year-old son. He called himself Ditso, and took pride in being unwashed, unironed, and unshorn. He and his friends were a great annoyance to the neighbors with their playing of namable and unnamable instruments. Work was beneath Ditso, but he was behind in payments on an electric guitar, and he baby-sat solely to keep the instrument company at bay. He charged seventy-five cents an hour instead of the fifty her high-school girls were satisfied with.

Beany's book club laughed uproariously when she explained her early leavetaking, "I have to get my sitter off the premises, and his litter cleaned up before Carl comes home."

"You mean your sitter doesn't do anything but sit?"

"*Slumps.* In a deck chair with a guitar or zither or guess-what draped across his middle. He not only does nothing for the children, but he bellows at them to bring him cold drinks out of the ice box. And they do. There'll be a circle of empty bottles, cigarette butts, and spilled potato chips around his chair for me to clean up quick. You can imagine how long he'd last with Carl." The members who knew Carlton laughed even more heartily.

And on each return from her book club or from a bridal or baby shower for an old schoolmate, Beany would lift the lid of the jewelry box and, to the tune of "In the Gloaming, oh my Darling," put into Ditso's unwashed palm the equivalent of perhaps a foot of living-room rug.

Wonderful McNally. She was someone for Beany to turn to in her grief over Kay, in her anxiety to do right by Jodey. McNally was sympathetic, comforting. She was a good listener. But she never talked about herself.

On one of those visits to the red stone house, McNally introduced Beany to the gray-haired, businesslike Alice Henderson, cashier at the Buckeye Bar and Grill.

"I'm a roomer here," the woman explained.

"Roomer!" McNally mocked fondly. "She's my Mrs. Grundy, business manager, and slave driver all rolled into one."

Later, when McNally was talking to a roomer upstairs, Mrs. Henderson confided to Beany, "I worry about her. Sometimes, I feel I started an avalanche I can't stop. When her mother died—and oh, Mrs. Buell, you can't imagine the physical and mental wreck Linda McNally was—I urged her to take a job at the Buckeye, just to get her out of this house of sickness and sorrow, and to be with people. I never dreamed but that, once she got hold of herself, she'd see about a schoolteaching job."

"I'm sure she will this fall."

The woman shook her head. "You have to apply ahead, you know. And then—well, there again, she was so broke, so weighted down with debts—I urged her to fix up these rooms and rent them. But I didn't mean for her to work, work, work till she's barely able to drag herself to bed at night."

McNally was now coming down the stairs, and Alice Henderson added swiftly, "See if you can talk sense to her, Mrs. Buell. You're her own age; maybe she'll listen to you."

Beany tried that very day. While her two were busy climbing up the stairs and bumping down, she helped McNally rip the cream-colored sateen lining out of a pair of dark draperies. McNally thought that curtains made from the lining would render an upstairs room less dark.

As they snipped threads, Beany asked in what she hoped was a conversational tone, "I suppose you're planning on teaching kindergarten when school opens this fall?"

"No, I'm not. Should I trim these curtains with fringe or a ruffle to sort of dress them up?"

"Fringe is pretty expensive. A ruffle of bright print

would be pretty. You don't mean that you're going to keep on waiting tables at the Buckeye?"

"I like waiting tables at the Buckeye."

"But, McNally, all those years of education courses, all those papers you wrote. And Peggy said *you* were the only practice teacher Maria Godwin kept asking for. You can't let all that go down the drain."

McNally said with her down-twisted smile, "When something goes sour, you might as well let it go down the drain." She held up first one length of lining and then the other. "Look at how sun-streaked they are. Do you suppose if I hung them out in whatever sun I can find in our shaded yard, they'd fade out evenly?"

It was her way of putting up a sign about her personal affairs: "Private Property. Keep Off."

Beany could only obey the sign. She said, "Here, I'll take the pieces home and put a strong bleach in the wash water, and then hang them in our back yard where there's more sun than we know what to do with."

When Joe Collins brought Jodey back after his biting the landlady's granddaughter's foot, he had insisted on paying for Jodey's "keep." Beany had shaken her head, "Oh no, no—I wouldn't feel right." Carlton, too, had said, "Don't worry about it now, Joe. You get out from under your debts." He meant Kay's doctor, hospital, and funeral expenses, not covered by insurance.

Joe was impulsively generous. One evening he stopped after work with two tickets for the theater at

Acacia Gardens. "One of my customers tells me it's a riot, so I got these for you two. I'll stay and herd the kids, so you can go with a clear conscience."

He was so pleased with himself that neither Beany nor Carlton had the heart to tell him that this was the evening Carlton planned to wade through thick law books in search of a precedent to guide him in a case tomorrow. They drove to Acacia Gardens, far over on the north side of the city, laughed through the comedy, and drove home. Carlton then settled down with his page-turning and note-taking until three in the morning.

On another day Joe, even more boyishly delighted with his gift, brought out a portable wading pool for the children. He set it up, filled it from the hose, and said, "There now, Beany. This will keep the three busy and cool and out of your hair."

Famous last words! For now she had all the children on Laurel Lane in her hair. The rough play of the big and bossy ones made it hard on the smaller toddlers. Twice Beany had to rescue Mary Liz, who had been pushed down in a water fight and was strangling and gulping for breath.

And these older children ganged up on Jodey. They resented his belligerence—a belligerence which, Beany knew, was outer covering for his fear. When they crowded him, he turned the hose on them. They, in turn, wrested it from him and doused him and everything in sight, including the washing on the line, with a strong spray of water.

After about ten days of this, Carlton returned one

late afternoon to find the back yard a noisy, water-splashed bedlam, and a frantic Beany mopping up water on the patio. He sent all the children scampering, except three named Jodey, Mister, and Mary Liz. He pulled out the plug, which held the water in the green receptacle, and said grimly as he tossed it up and down in his palm, "For all intents and purposes, *this* is lost."

He had come home early because tonight was the opening of the lighted baseball field on which his own Bombshells would play the first game. For two years he had worked on a committee that met with and prodded the city fathers into providing this lighted field for the Young America teams of the state.

Beany had completely forgotten that this was *the* big night. Carlton said, "There'll be the usual fanfare with a band and souvenirs. The governor is to turn on the floodlights, and the mayor will toss the first ball. We'd better go early on account of the parking. Better take a blanket in case Mary Liz goes to sleep."

"Oh, Carl, you know how Jodey is in a crowd."

"You knew this was coming up," he said crossly. "Didn't you line up Ditso to stay with him?"

She was ashamed to confess she had completely forgotten. "Wednesday night is sacred for Ditso," she excused herself. "He and his cronies have started a Jug Band, and this is their night to practice. You go, Carl," she urged. "I suppose you and your committee will stand up and take a bow. I'll wait up, and you can tell me all about it."

She was hard put to find night clothes for the children because of the water fight reaching the clothes on the line. She herself had to don Carlton's shirt with the hacked-off sleeves.

She wouldn't go to bed. Instead, she would doze briefly on the couch, and be wideawake and rested when Carlton returned. . . . In her heavy sleep, she dreamed of loud thumping on the front door. And then of a gate's clicking, and of the French door's opening and someone coming in and trying to quiet Thumper, and then that someone was bending over and saying, "Beany, Beany, if you're not dead, wake up!"

She jerked herself up on the couch. Even then it took a minute or two for her to place *who* she was and *where* she was, and *who* her husband was and *why* he was standing there.

"Did your Bombshells win?" she asked with bright but false interest.

"Tie." He stood looking down at her sleep-drenched figure. "Jodey's too much for you. He's that much too much with everything else."

"Oh, no, Carl, honest—it's just that today was murder with all those little honyaks battling and soaking everything." And then, feeling guilty because she had meant to be waiting with sandwiches, cold drinks, and consuming interest in his evening, she talked swiftly, "Don't you remember how you drilled me unmercifully in swimming so I could pass the water-safety test and how—?"

"I remember your being so mad at me you tried to drown me."

136

"I was mad because you were such an unsympathetic cuss. When I'd be out of breath and my muscles were aching, you'd say, 'That's part of building up muscle strength.'"

"The next time Joe Collins stops to see Jodey, have him come out and have dinner with us, and let's talk over—"

"He's putting in all the extra time he can. Seven to seven, most days. And then remember how I had to cram on Applied Anatomy and Kinesiology in college? All I have to do yet is say *Kinesiology* to get a headache. You'd drill me on it, and when I'd say my brain hurt, you'd say the same thing—and with the same lack of sympathy, 'That's your mental muscles stretching.' Well, you have to build up patience and coping muscles, too."

She wished he'd say, "I get the point. As soon as your coping muscles strengthen, you'll breeze through your days and be fresh as a daisy at night." Instead he said, "On your feet, Cutty Sark, and muscle down the hall to bed."

The next day when Joe Collins stopped briefly on Laurel Lane, Beany didn't even mention his coming to dinner to talk over plans for Jodey. Another matter diverted her whole attention.

Joe brought, as usual, a carton of soft drinks. "And here's something else, so the three of you can have yourselves a party." He reached back to the high seat of the truck for a box, and took off the lid. "Look there. Cupcakes all pink and fancied up."

Beany looked at the toothsome array of cupcakes with their generous daubs of garish pink icing and those purplish lumps that were bits of strawberry jam. She breathed out, "Yvonne made those."

"Yeah, Vonnie. That's right. I forgot you met her, Beany. She's from Peachtree, too," he added innocently, "and it's such a little burg that everybody feels sort of family to everybody else. Vonnie says when she feels lonely, it helps her to stir up something. And then, when she makes things like this, she says she has to think up someone to give them to. So she called me up and asked if I could stop by. That was last night. I ate one on my route, but I'm not much for sweet stuff."

That sly, never-say-die Yvonne letting no grass grow under her determined feet. And old bumbling, naïve Joe, thinking her only interest was that of a fellow Peachtreeite in the big city. He went on, "She said she knew what a bad time I was going through. And any time I felt like talking about Cooky and old times, to come up."

Beany's soul groaned. That, from the girl who called Jodey a monster and Kay a millstone around Joe's neck.

❦ 14 ❧

Every Fourth of July since Beany and Carlton had been married, they had packed the "diamond brooch" —often crowding in bottled formula and canned baby food—and set out for the mountains. But this Fourth the metal hamper went right on collecting dust on the shelf in the garage.

The days were hotter, and the house, with the front door closed and bolted, stuffier.

Beany's grief for Kay didn't lessen. And with it was her longing to do for Jodey, to bring him out from under his dark cloud. Somehow the pattern in the whole Beany-Kay relationship was of Beany, the protector, the helper of the gentle, idealistic Kay through her bad times. So Beany was driven by a sense of something unfinished, of a trust unfulfilled.

By now Ditso's Jug Band was having tryouts at some of the coffee houses. The last time Beany asked him to baby-sit, his contemporaries came, too, with their washboards, bull fiddles, and bongo drums, and practiced on the Buell patio. Their three young charges

139

were delighted, but Thumper crawled under the bed in the master bedroom, and Mrs. Kincaid, next door, went shopping.

More and more, Beany found herself eeling out of going places. It meant hurrying home even earlier to an even greater shambles, and a more depleted refrigerator. And these weary days nothing seemed worth the effort.

She gave trumped-up excuses: she had called the plumber and she wasn't sure when he would arrive— "You know how it is." Or she was expecting her sister Mary Fred and her husband down from Wyoming.

Carlton overheard her one morning making excuses for not going to her book club luncheon that day. "What's this about a stuffed-up sink and a plumber to the rescue?"

Beany flushed guiltily. "I had to have some excuse. The meeting is at Joyce's, and it'll be crowded, and her house is so hot—and she always serves one of those sticky-sweet marshmallow salads, and the last time I was there her Peke nipped me on the shin."

"But it's your turn to give a book review, you said."

"That's all right. They can always fill in. No one listens anyway."

"I'll bet you didn't even read your book."

She hadn't. She'd had neither the time nor energy to, much less make notes for a lucid summing up. "No, I didn't. It's by O'Hara, and you said yourself you had yet to find a faithful wife or husband in a book by him. Every time I read one of his, I feel as though I haven't lived because I've never had an illicit love affair or gone to a psychiatrist."

"You have the illicit love affair, and I'll guarantee the psychiatrist," he said. He cupped her chin in his hand and kissed her freckled nose. "I'm not as worried about the love affair as I am of your getting cabin fever."

Later, when he and Uncle Matthew were leaving, Carlton lingered to ask, "Don't you think you could take a chance on leaving the door open with just the screen latched?"

Beany evaded, "Yes, maybe we could."

She was enough on the defensive, since Carlton had said Jodey was too much for her, that she didn't tell him everything. She *had* left the door unbolted a few days before. And Jodey had heard a truck rumbling past that he mistook for the Bartell truck and had gone plummeting down Laurel Lane.

Beany caught him at the end of two long blocks. This time when she panted out, "Jodey, why did you run away?" he answered, "I thought it was Dad. It rattled just like his truck."

So Beany kept the heavy door bolted. And to the invitations to poolside brunches, matinees at Acacia Gardens, or going-away parties, she dusted off the excuse of the expected plumber or the expected visitors from Big Basin.

By one of life's coincidences, she was on the phone using the latter, when there came an impatient pounding at the door, and she said, "Wait just a minute till

I let someone in." Mary Fred and Ander came in with such noisy greetings that she silenced them with a panicky, "Sh-h-h, please. I'm just telling somebody I'm expecting you day after tomorrow." She added on a sigh, "I know it's a sin to lie like this, but it's such a hopeless job trying to explain about getting a baby sitter for poor Jodey."

The minute Beany replaced the phone, Ander was asking, "How is he, Beany? I've been wanting to get down, but we've had so many new babies and broken bones. Did Jodey go through a bad time after the funeral?"

Mary Fred broke in, "We came down because I've been asked to ride Sir Echo in the Shriners' Palomino Parade. You know the one they have at the stadium every Colorado Day. The field manager wants to show me the patterns of the figure eights, and the Virginia reel, and where my position is."

Beany answered Ander, "Yes, for awhile he was both a lost soul and Satan on horseback. But he's a lot better now."

The children came in from the back yard. The one under discussion stood, sober and aloof, while Mary Liz showed the visitors her new ruffled pants of which she was unduly proud.

Ander asked Beany, "Doesn't a certain party ever l-a-u-g-h?"

"No. But, at times, almost a s-m-i-l-e." It was usually when Mary Liz twisted her words, like ice-cone cream or jack-cracker, that a faint twitch of smile came to his lips.

Again Jodey greeted Ander with, "My dad's big-ger'n you," and he answered with, "You bet he is."

The little boy stood his distance from Mary Fred, even as he did with Mrs. Kincaid and Beany's step-mother, but he warmed to Ander and showed him the coffee can Miss McNally had let him paint.

Ander asked Jodey if he would like to go with him while he did some errands, and Jodey said yes. Beany left the front door open to gather what little western breeze was stirring.

Ander and Jodey returned about an hour later. Neither one looked as though the ride had been relax-ing, and Jodey's eyes had their old haunted shadow. Beany had only to say, "Take your nap now, honey," for him to dart into the room where Mary Liz was already asleep and shut the door.

In the kitchen Ander ran cold water for a drink. Everything had gone fine for a while, he told Beany. They had stopped at the park, and Jodey had fed the ducks popcorn. He had talked freely about everything —but not about Peachtree or anyone there.

Then Ander had driven on to Colorado General Hospital to pick up a lab report for the doctor he worked with in Big Basin. "Beany, it was pitiful. I no sooner stopped at the curb than Jodey screamed out, 'It's a hospital!' and tried to leap out of the car. I had to hold him tight. He was like a little trapped animal, shaking all over. I saw there was no chance of either taking him in with me or of leaving him in the car, so I came home."

He ran another glass of water and drained it. "I

remember Joe saying something about Jodey sitting in the car while he was in the hospital with Kay. Didn't he say they couldn't get him within a mile of a hospital?"

"Yes. And the next day when I took him to see his mother, I fairly had to drag him in. Like you, I could feel him shaking inside. But I thought it would comfort him to see Kay. It didn't." She told of his beating on the bed and screaming for his mother to come home, and of his bolting into the bathroom when the nurse appeared. "Kay said it was the white uniform that scared him. And she was right, because when Eudora Holden brought Kay's belongings here, Jodey wasn't afraid of her."

Mary Fred called from the living room, "Ander, we have to get over to the stadium so I can go into a huddle about my position in the different formations. Between three and four, the letter said."

Ander turned, and looked at her over the low partition as though he had forgotten there was such a thing as an upcoming horse show called the Palomino Parade. "Yes, yes, we'll go in a minute. Beany, tell me everything Kay told you about Jodey and his hospital experience."

She gave him all the details: Jodey's broken shoulder and Joe's being away with the football team for the Thanksgiving game. "Kay wanted to stay with Jodey at the hospital. He was only about fourteen months old, and he'd never been away from home before. But the hospital wouldn't let her."

144

"That's at Peachtree, right? Was he in a room with other children?"

"Yes, with two or three others. Kay said he came back from the hospital a different child than he went in. Before the cast was off his shoulder, he was running away, and saying no, no, no to everything. Kay was so weak from a miscarriage, she couldn't be on her feet much so Grandpa Jethro took over. You saw what an opinionated little banty rooster he is, and he was sure all Jodey needed was a blistered behind."

"God help us," Ander breathed.

"And then Joe's sister, the Aline you met here, would take him off Kay's hands for a while. You heard her say she didn't hold with pampering children. So when Jodey ran away, she tied him to the clothesline."

Ander's listening grunt was one of pain.

"Kay blamed herself. She felt that if she had only been strong enough to have the sole care of Jodey, he'd have straightened out."

"Yes, and she's right. He could have built up his security if he'd known she was always there to turn to. That's why Joe is so important to him." He turned the cold water on again. This time he cupped it in his hands and, bending over, soused it over his face. He shook it out of his eyes. "No, no, I don't need a towel," he said.

Just so would a cowhand cool himself off after a hot, worrying ride, Beany thought.

"Yes, something frightening happened at the hospital. If he was only fourteen months old, he was old enough to feel the terror, but not old enough to understand it, or talk about it." Another thoughtful pause. "I wish—Lord, I wish I had time to go into the whole case and spend more time with the boy." He was pacing the length of kitchen and service room. He stopped to call over the partition, "Tell you what, Mary Fred, I'll drop you off at the stadium, and then go back to Colorado General and get the lab report. I want to see who's in charge of the Child Psychiatric Division now and, if I get a chance, talk to him about Jodey."

They set out together.

The sun was starting its drop behind the western mountains when Mary Fred returned home afoot from the stadium. "Just a nice constitutional," she said with thin-lipped exasperation because Ander had failed to pick her up.

The sun was much lower when he returned. Carlton called him to come in and have dinner. No, Ander said, he'd have to step on it so he could take care of the outpatients at the hospital in Big Basin. "Tell Mary Fred to come on."

This time it was Mary Fred, the aggrieved wife, who sat in glum silence on the ride home, and Ander who talked. He had found that a Dr. Nelson, who had been at Johns Hopkins with him, was one of the staff in pediatric mental health at Colorado General. "Nels, we used to call him. He was always a tactless Swede. Maybe he is yet with grownups, but I sat there and observed his handling of those mixed-up kids, and he was all gentleness, understanding. I got so interested, I almost forgot the outpatients at Big Basin."

"I'm glad you remembered them, even if you forgot your wife who was waiting at the stadium. And turning down offers of a ride with, 'Thank you, but my husband is coming for me.'"

"I'm sorry, Mary Fred," he said placatingly. "Tell me about your horse show."

"It's only about two weeks away—Colorado Day. It'll start at eleven in the morning. Supposed to take an hour and a half, but they can never pull it off in that. It's the usual formations. After the Virginia reel, we spell out *Colorado*. Sir Echo and I will be one of two to make the short end of the L."

She went on talking. But he wasn't listening. He was looking ahead at the road, completely engrossed in his own thoughts.

❦ 15 ❧

On Friday morning, following the Erharts' visit, Beany sang lustily as she ran an iron over the dripdry shirt Carlton was waiting to put on. Today was the day Buell and Buell expected a decision on a water-rights case that had been dragging on for weeks. He and Uncle Matthew departed hastily.

Yes, rested from a long night's sleep, Beany felt her coping muscles, like the muscles in the arms of the village smith, were strong as iron bands. When Mister, surveying his breakfast egg, said, "I wish we'd have eggs that look like little boats with yellow pillows in them," she laughed, rubbed noses with him, and promised, "Righto, Mister William James, we'll have boats with pillows in them for lunch," and promptly put on eggs to boil for deviling.

And when her father phoned and said, "I hope you haven't forgotten whose birthday this is," she laughed again, and said, "Miss Hewlitt's. I did forget, but I'll stir up a cake and take it right out to her."

Miss Hewlitt was a retired lit. teacher who had

taught Martie Malone, and all four of the Malone children. How often had Beany squirmed in her class at Harkness High, when the lit. teacher told her captive audience of Martie Malone's writing genius and of her getting him his first newspaper job. Then she would tell of Johnny Malone, his gifted son, whom she had also nurtured. It was all true, too.

Miss Hewlitt was a blunt-spoken woman who had sought to instill a love of poetry in her students, and had succeeded with a few. She was a collector of dolls, and was now deaf (though she denied it) and had arthritic knees (which she couldn't deny, because a cane was necessary).

"Can you go out with me?" Beany asked her father.

No, he couldn't make it. He was leaving right away for a press conference. But would Beany be a lamb and pick up the roses he had ordered at the Boulevard Flower Shop? "I'm glad you're taking her a cake, Beany. She'd be lost if she couldn't serve it at the birthday gathering of her old cronies this afternoon, and brag about it."

Beany's high spirits remained undaunted at finding neither cake nor icing mix in the cupboard. She'd make what Mister called a "Scratch Cake," because he'd heard her say she made it from scratch.

When the cake batter was ready, she rattled through every cupboard without finding her third layer-cake pan. Extending her search to the sandbox, she unearthed it, dented and rusted. She was a half hour scouring it and trying to pound out the dents.

She put on sugar and water to cook for her old

reliable seven-minute icing. Be nice to color it pink. She thought instantly of those violent pink cupcakes that had been used as bait for Joe Collins. The thought of Yvonne silenced her singing to the whirr of the egg-beater in the frothy whites.

Both Thumper's dog ears and Jodey's little boy ears always recognized that certain rumble and clank of the Bartell truck coming down Laurel Lane. Time out from the cake baking while Beany opened the door, and the three children and dog scampered across the lawn. Beany followed.

Joe put into Jodey's hands a carton of six bottles, another into Mister's, and a small packet of candy for Mary Liz. "Honey drops for a honey babe," he said, and swung her high in the air.

He couldn't give any rides around the block today, for every customer was screaming for a rush delivery. But tomorrow, he'd try to manage it. With those pink-frosted cupcakes still in mind, Beany delayed him by questions as to whether he was still working late and what he had been doing. She meant, "Have you seen that wily Yvonne?" He answered innocently enough —but she still didn't know.

But she did know the minute she herded the children through the front door that the syrup for her own pink frosting had burned black. Oh, dear, she'd have to soak the pan in the sink, and start all over again with more sugar and water.

The layer in the warped pan wouldn't come out in one piece—or even in *two*. It was a nerve-wracking chore, fitting the pieces together and frosting over the cracks. The morning was well gone before she spaced the candles over the *pale* pink icing: H—H, meaning Hewlitt and Harkness. Then five candles in a row, representing the five Malones Miss Hewlitt had taught.

On previous birthdays Beany had taken the children. But you never knew about Jodey. He might refuse to get out of the car. He might go in to Miss Hewlitt's with his belligerent scowl, which would lead to her prying into the why of it. It was hard enough to explain to someone with good hearing, much less to someone who had to be yelled at.

Ditso was home when she phoned to ask if he would baby-sit. Sure, sure, he'd be over on the double. He'd leave word for Sacko to come over, too. "We're having a tryout at the Sad Onion tonight, and we got to practice."

Beany decided it would be simpler all around to leave Mister and Mary Liz with him.

Ditso came with his "little old brown jug" and demonstrated the *woo-ooo* sound he could produce by slanting his blowing breath a certain way into and across its opening. "Man, you'd be surprised at how hard it is to track down a little old brown jug like this. Took me four days."

"Yes, I imagine." She eased the top of the cake box over the cake. "They've used *glass* jugs as long as I can remember. I won't be gone long. Hold the door open for me, please, Ditso, and then fasten it."

"Stop *at* the Boulevard Flower Shop," her father had said. Because of traffic and parked cars on the busy thoroughfare, she had to park on a side street two blocks away. The sun beat hotly down on her as she walked to it, and back with the long florist's box under her arm.

She had another parking problem at Miss Hewlitt's. Her small house had once been on the outskirts of the city, but now the city had grown out to and past it, and a hospital was built across the street. Parking had been no problem when in Beany's teens, Miss Hewlitt gave a Get-Acquainted for the Literary Society. This close to noon, Beany drove around the block twice before she took a chance on a space across the street that said, "For Doctors Only."

At Miss Hewlitt's door, she had a hard time making her presence known. The TV, going full blast inside evidently drowned out the bell's ringing. Beany deposited cake box and flowers on the floor, and pounded loud and long before the old schoolteacher, whiter of hair and rounder of shoulders, opened the door. "Beany! You Malones are like elephants—you never forget."

The same sunless stuffiness that Beany remembered. The same crowded clutter, with dolls overflowing from the living room into dining room and bedroom. Dolls from Hungary, Spain, China. A ballet dancer, a doll in Scottish kilts. Beany wanted to ask if the doll whose head was a red-cheeked apple had shriveled away, but she dared not get Miss Hewlitt started on her doll family.

Beany said, "I'll take the cake into the kitchen, and

find a vase for the flowers. Are your birthday friends coming?"

"The old relics? Yes, this afternoon. There were ten—no, eleven of us—when we started celebrating birthdays. Now there are only three besides me."

"Ah, I'm sorry."

"Don't be. We've all had our three-score and ten —and a few extra, to boot. Old withered leaves can't hang onto the tree forever. That white vase there, if you can reach it."

Beany filled the vase with water, and Miss Hewlitt arranged the long-stemmed red roses. "Willful extravagance, when back yards are full of flowers," the old teacher said with pleased tch-tchs. "Martie used to bring me roses when he couldn't afford but three or four." She couldn't find her magnifying glass, so Beany read the card which pleased her even more, "To a very important woman in my life."

Johnny Malone had sent a scarf from Texas with long-horned steers and bucking horses on it. Beany doubted that Miss Hewlitt would ever wear it, but she would show it off to her friends this afternoon.

It had been hard to get into the house, and it was even harder to get out. Miss Hewlitt had to hear all about every member of the family. Her hearing might be dulled, but her mind was still sharp.

"What did Kay die of?"

"She had leukemia, but it was her heart that failed all of a sudden."

"I never thought that ninny of a mother gave her

enough to eat. Tell me about her little boy that you're taking care of."

"Jodey's going on five. He has blond hair like Kay's."

Oh-oh! The words "blond hair" were a mistake. For Miss Hewlitt had to show Beany the blond boy doll and its twin sister with flaxen braids which a friend had brought her from Holland. "Did you know, Beany, that the Netherlands exported dolls first? They manufactured them long before Great Britain did. Flanders babies, they were called."

The cuckoo clock was cuckooing twelve times when Beany started for the door. At that, it took her twenty minutes to edge through it and down the front steps.

"Old women talk too much," Miss Hewlitt even called after her. Beany, feeling somehow guilty to be hurrying away, vowed that *someday* she'd come and give time to noticing the homespun petticoat on the Irish doll and the real lace mantilla on the Spanish one.

At home, she again had to pound loud and long on her own door, and hear Thumper's agonized whimpers, before it was opened by Ditso. "Couldn't hear you on the patio. We thought it'd be cooler out there, but we thought wrong."

She stopped and looked in the refrigerator for one of the soft drinks Joe Collins had left. Every one of the twelve bottles was gone. She drank cold water instead, feeling a hurting trip hammer in her temple as she did so.

What a messy kitchen she had left, complete with burnt-sugar smell. She walked on through the living

154

room—also messy. But the patio was a shambles. Empty bottles, crunchy potato chips and Fritos underfoot, shoes and socks Ditso and Sacko had sloughed off; and one sodden small heap that was Mary Liz's ruffled pants, discarded, no doubt, because of their wet discomfort. A huge bull fiddle occupied the glider. *So help me, if I ever call on Ditso again. I'll stay home forever.*

Mister was sitting on the ground beside Sacko, holding up a slide whistle. "Listen to how I can play," he said happily, and tootled shrilly on it.

Jodey, not to be outdone, went hurrying over to the somewhat unsteady table and Ditso's brown jug sitting on a corner of it. "I can blow on a jug," he bragged, and reached for it.

Beany, thinking only of how hard it had been for Ditso to procure that brown jug, and of how fatal it would be if it were dropped on the brick floor, moved swiftly toward Jodey to take it from him. She didn't see the tray full of melting ice cubes on the floor. She tripped over it and fell on her knees, bumping into Jodey and the jug. The result was that instead of rescuing the jug, she knocked it out of his hands and it crashed onto the brick floor.

There was a moment of stunned silence broken by Mary Liz's wailing and Mister's saying, "The top half didn't hardly break at all."

Ditso didn't upbraid either Beany or Jodey as she expected. He only said in a voice of doom, "Us on tonight at the Onion—and no jug." But Sacko turned on Jodey. "Now look what happened! How many times did we tell you to keep your creepy hands off our stuff?"

Beany pulled a stricken Jodey to her. "He didn't do it—*I* did. Blame me. But, Ditso, I think I can locate another one for you. My husband's mother was a great one to save things. She's got scads of old-time stuff in their basement and attic. She isn't there now, but I'll phone and ask the renters if we can go down and look for one."

She dialed the familiar number of the ivy-covered Buell house, which Dulcie called a mausoleum. There was no answer. She phoned her own home next door, and Adair informed her that the professor who rented the Buell house had gone on a two-week vacation with his family. "The place is locked up tighter than a drum."

Beany sat on at the phone and, starting with Goodwill, went down the list of salvage stores. Not one had a brown jug. "We used to have more than we knew what to do with, lady, but I haven't seen one in I couldn't tell you when."

"Ditso, couldn't you use a glass jug? I noticed one out in our garage."

He guessed you could blow music on it just the same, he said gloomily, but Sacko derided, "Now how would that look for fellows in plaid shirts and runover boots to h'ist a glass jug?"

Beany said, "If we could make a glass jug look like a brown one, would that do? We used to cover jars and bottles with this brown masking tape at the Neighborhood House. And they looked just like pottery."

156

They reckoned it would *have* to do.

The glass jug in the garage held vile-smelling paint remover. She had other half-gallon syrup ones, but they had no handle to crook a finger in.

She emptied the paint remover into something else, and scrubbed out the jug with bottle brush and strong soap solution again and again. The children watched with interest, and the musicians with cynicism, while she cut strips of brown gummed tape, wet them with a sponge, and wrapped them around and around the glass surface.

And at last, Ditso took her handiwork which he admitted grudgingly might pass for a brown jug from a distance. She counted out his baby-sitting pay to the wistful melody of "In the Gloaming, Oh, my darling." *In the living room, Oh, my darling, will there ever be a rug?*

Nothing would do for Jodey and Mister, but that they, too, must make themselves brown jugs out of glass ones to blow on. Beany gave them each a corn-syrup, handless one. Each held jealously to a roll of tape. "After your naps, you can cover them," she said. "Come on now and eat your lunch."

Strange, how children are always more perverse when a mother is driven and exhausted. Jodey insisted on cutting some strips of gummed paper. Mister complained, "You *said* we could have egg boats with yellow pillows in them," and she snapped, "Oh, for heaven's sake, it's two hours past your lunchtime now. Eat them plain and hush."

And Mary Liz refused to sit in her high chair. Beany

gave in, and let her occupy one of the stools at the snack bar with the boys. Beany peeled herself an egg, and gulped it down. It seemed to lump itself in her gullet.

Armed with broom and dustpan, she went out to the patio. It wasn't until she hunkered down to brush up the shards of the pottery jug, that she realized one knee had been skinned when she fell here on the brick floor and that her whole body felt wrenched and jolted. But a good soaking in a hot tub would take care of that.

The minute she heard the screams in the kitchen she knew what had happened. Mary Liz had fallen off the stool. "She went part way to sleep," Mister explained over the din.

It took a half hour of rocking and soothing before Mary Liz's tearful eyes closed for her nap.

☙ 16 ☙

As Beany straightened up, after easing Mary Liz into her crib, the trip hammer was pounding viciously in her temple. Another time she would have laughed to see Jodey on his cot, clutching his jug with one hand and strips of brown tape with the other, while he pretended to be asleep. But today she said shortly, "You're not to touch that jug until you have a nap."

She couldn't take time for her soaking bath—not with the breakfast, cake-baking, and luncheon dishes still to be done, and the patio still unpicked up. She would settle for an aspirin, a coating of salve on her sore knee, and a rest on the living-room couch for— Oh, a half hour would make a new woman out of her.

She was reaching for the aspirin on the shelf over the sink, when she heard a car stopping in front. She saw through the kitchen window the Trighorn pickup and Dulcie bouncing out of it. Oh, no! Not this afternoon. How could she endure Dulcie's remarks about a living room looking like "poor white" without a carpet? Or her telling her how Jodey should be handled?

She didn't even want to hear about the Dames' Club. For a craven moment, she wondered if she could pretend she wasn't home. But besides it's being a scurvy trick, Dulcie would probably pound on the door until she wakened the children.

Beany slid off the high bolt and opened the door.

"Honestly!" Dulcie greeted her, "All this clunking of bolts. Like Alcatraz. Wouldn't it be a lot simpler just to hobble Jodey and leave the door open? Is he still so bratty?"

"He was never bratty. But he's coming out of his shyness—"

"Shyness, my eye. I've got another name for it."

Beany changed the subject. "I'm about six jumps behind, because I took a birthday cake out to Miss Hewlitt. You remember her? She taught us lit. at Harkness?"

"I remember her telling me to wash the axle grease off my eyes. I came out to use your sewing machine. Trig's putting in a deep freeze on our back porch, and he had to turn our electricity off."

Beany got her machine from the hall closet, and set it up on a card table in the living room. Dulcie reached into her shopping bag, and shook out what Beany saw was a basted-together dress. The Dames' Club, said Dulcie, was going to the Saturday matinee at Acacia Gardens tomorrow, and she wanted a new dress to wear.

"All my summer clothes looked so washed-out and muckle-dun. Something new is always a shot in the arm for me. All the summer goods are on sale now. You go down and get a dress length, and I'll make it for you."

"Thanks, Dulcie, but I don't need a dress."

"You need something for darn sure. You look like the tag end of a hard winter. There's just no sense in a girl letting herself go to seed."

Inwardly Beany found herself saying to Kay, "Now Dulcie is raking me over the coals for letting myself go to seed." . . . With a jolt she remembered. Never again would she and Kay laugh over Dulcie's bluntness or bragging. The tears that had been close to the surface since the icing burned this morning pushed to her eyes. She hurried to the kitchen, muttering that she'd make some iced tea.

Good heavens, no ice cubes. She had stumbled over that one tray on the patio, but she had supposed the other was full and nesting in the refrigerator. She found it *under* the glider, and carried it in along with the one that had caused her skinned knee and Ditso's smashed jug. She filled both, and slid them into the freezer compartment with a panicky glance at the clock. Would the water be ice in time for Uncle Matthew to rattle it in his "two fingers of Scotch"?

"Sorry, Dulcie, no iced tea. No ice."

"That's something we'll never run out of. You ought to see this giant freezer Trig is putting in."

While the machine hummed, Beany moved with aimless inefficiency from one room to another. She didn't shake the rumpled scatter rugs and lay them flat; that might call Dulcie's attention to the needed but absent rug.

Dulcie said, "There now, I've finished the stitching."

Beany heard her with wondrous relief. She could still manage *ten* minutes on the couch with the damp washcloth over her eyes and salve on her knee.

Dulcie was holding her garment up to her. There was nothing washed-out or "muckle-dun" about its electric blues, greens, and oranges. "They call this reptile print." Suddenly the unsure-of-herself little girl came through. "Beany, do you think it looks loud—and cheap?"

It was this running-scared side of Dulcie that had first won Beany's sympathy and friendship. "Not on you, Dulcie. You can get away with it. You're the bird-of-paradise type."

Dulcie was shucking off her shirt and shorts, squirming her arms and head through the sleeves and neck of the reptile print. Her muffled words were, "Will you turn up the hem for me while I'm here? Then I can whip it in by hand this evening. Get your yardstick and pins."

Good-bye ten minutes on the couch with damp washcloth and salve.

Beany was looking for the yardstick and not finding it, when Jodey emerged from his room with his jug and strips of gummed tape. Seeing Dulcie, with whom he was never comfortable, he took himself and project to the bathroom.

She was looking for a piece of cardboard to use in lieu of the missing yardstick, when Mister also appeared on the scene with his syrup container and announced, "I can do mine all by my ownself."

The skinned knee asserted itself again when Beany

tried to kneel for measuring Dulcie's hem. She had to sit on the floor while Dulcie pivoted slowly and confided, "None of the Dames are flashy dressers. They're a lot different from me. Now you'd fit right in, Beany, because you've been to college. They talk about books and writers I never even heard of. I thought George Sand was a man. I thought Colette was the name of a book. Do you know I haven't read a book since I left Harkness? It was *Lady of the Lake* that finished me off. I don't tell them that I didn't even graduate from Harkness High. And they've all traveled more than I have."

"Don't forget your bragging to me the first time I saw you that you were seventeen and had lived in seventeen different places."

"Oh sure. All those dumps Dad dragged poor old Mom and me to when he was chasing uranium. Remember how Mary Fred was always spouting psychology and how she once said that a girl who was crazy about her father always married a man *like* him?"

"That figures," Beany muttered around the pins in her mouth. "My father couldn't even put a hanger on the back of one of Adair's pictures. And then I married a man that can't hit a nail on the first try."

"And Mary Fred said that a girl that didn't look up to her father married just the—she had some big two-bit word—"

"Antithesis."

"That's it. And that figures too. Because Trig is certainly as antith—as you can get from my old man."

"Walk away, Dulcie, and let's see. Mister, you're

getting your tape too wet. You're washing the glue off it."

As Dulcie stepped away, her eyes rested on the large oil over Beany's fireplace. It was Adair's painting of the Malone home on Barberry Street where the four children had lived from birth to marriage.

There were only three two-story houses on their side of the street in that block on Barberry. It was always amazing to Beany how Adair, with only the suggestion of the other two houses, had caught the preening prettiness of the green shutters, ruffled curtains, and gay window boxes of the one on the left, and the ordered, well-kept, even judicial uprightness of the ivy-covered red brick on the right where the Judge Buells lived—Dulcie's mausoleum. And how truly Adair's brush portrayed the wide-bosomed, open-doored Malone house, with its scuffed porch running around two sides and the chestnut tree's white blossoms lying, unraked, on the lawn.

Dulcie said, "One of the Dames has a picture as big as that on the wall of her family homestead in Maryland with what she calls 'trotters' in a field. I guess she wants everyone to know she's somebody."

"I just like looking at this one. Because those three houses have a sentimental link. Ander Erhart's aunt lived in the ruffly one, and you can see the hole in the Buell hedge where Carl and Johnny—and later, I—chased back and forth. . . . Dulcie, there's just one spot. Back up. There. Now hold your arms up, and I'll lift it over your head so you won't stick yourself."

And hurry into your shirt and shorts and go.

Here came Mary Liz, bright-eyed, smiling, and naked as a jaybird. She was very adept at taking clothes off, but not at putting them on. Beany got laboriously to her feet to find covering for her.

Suddenly Beany remembered the veal she should have taken from their freezer compartment this morning to thaw, in order to have breaded cutlets for the Buell dinner. Now she would have to hurry the process by putting the marbleized meat in a bowl and fitting the bowl on top of the simmering teakettle.

She did just that. She unlatched the door to let Dulcie out, and was told, "The next time I come, I'll bring you some of our fresh vegetables."

Jodey emerged from the bathroom with his jug almost covered. He *was* deft with his hands. "Is it time to put string on for a handle?" he asked.

"Cover up this one bare spot, and then I'll find the string for you."

A car was stopping in their driveway. *Oh, no,* again —*Oh, no!* Not Carlton and Uncle Matthew home early today!

Both men came in exuberant and triumphant. She felt it in her husband's kiss even before he said, "We won our case." (She had forgotten entirely about the dragged-out water-rights case.)

A strutting Uncle Matthew opened the cupboard and took down his bottle of pale amber liquid. Carlton yanked out an ice-cube tray, only to have the water slosh wetly over his front.

"I'm sorry they're not frozen," Beany apologized.

"There's a thin skeleton of ice around the edges," Carlton said. "Enough to cool a drink."

Mister was claiming his father's and uncle's attention with his jug. Jodey sat on the floor, eyeing Uncle Matthew as though he were about to snatch his prize from him. Jodey was never his best around the old gentleman, and he, in turn, had ideas about handling him that almost coincided with Dulcie's. Now, when the three grown-ups moved from the hall into the living room, Jodey scurried back to the bathroom and shut the door.

Beany hurriedly gathered up sponges and bowls, from which water had spilled, and straightened out the limp and lumpy rugs to cover the wettest spots. She snatched at pieces of wet gummed tape and found that most were stuck fast to the floor.

Uncle Matthew stood with his glass, holding forth about the judge's decision that had been the happy, but well-deserved, culmination of months of drudging, detailed, exacting labor. "Your husband covered himself with glory," he told Beany. She caught Carlton's wink that said, "How he loves those trite and flowery phrases!"

Uncle Matthew stopped talking and took a sip of his drink, in which the thin ghosts of ice had soon melted. Carlton said, "The clients insist on taking us out to dinner this evening to celebrate. To that new Rainbow Club by the race track. You know, where they serve dinner outdoors and the orchestra and dance floor is outside too."

"You and *me*?" Beany asked.

"Well, they asked me and my wife, and I can't think of any other wife."

Carl certainly was feeling on top of the world!

"Why don't you and Uncle Matthew go? I mean, you'll want to talk business, and I—"

Uncle Matthew broke in, "No, my dear, no. When it comes to the social end of it, I leave that to the younger generation. I'll pay for the baby-sitter, and feel it a privilege, so that you and your husband can make this a memorable and triumphant evening."

Another time the thought of dining under hanging lanterns and dancing under the stars would have sent her pulses racing. This whole worrisome, nettlesome day must have hardened her enjoyment arteries. "I don't know who we could get to baby-sit," she demurred. "This is McNally's week to work from four to midnight."

"There aren't many baby-sitters Jodey is happy with," Carlton explained to his uncle. "What about Ditso?"

"His Jug Band is having a tryout tonight at the Sad Onion. He and Sacko were here this morning while I took a cake to Miss Hewlitt. That's what knocked the bottom out of the whole day, because Jodey—I mean *I* broke Ditso's precious jug and had to produce a rather poor facsimile, and that's why this sudden rash of jug covering in our midst."

She could tell by the look on Uncle Matthew's face that he was about to launch into an oration on a woman's first duty belonging to her husband and chil-

167

dren, and so she raced on, "I wish you'd see their musical instruments. A washboard to thumpety-thump out the rhythm, and a piece of pipe they call a bangouza——"

"Beany, my dear, I don't believe you realize—"

"And they call themselves the Purple-footed Grape Stompers." She laughed as though this fact was inordinately hilarious. "They have dime-store harmonicas, and I tried blowing on Ditso's one day and, believe it or not, I could play 'Yankee Doodle.' A jug is something else again. Ditso says you have to be full of hot air to play one." She laughed even more hilariously.

"Beany, I must say something to you," pursued Uncle Matthew.

"Goodness, the string. We couldn't find jugs with handles, so I told Jodey and Mister we could make them out of twine." She started for the kitchen.

"Just a minute, Beany," the old gentleman said so firmly that she halted in the kitchen doorway. She cast a pleading look at Carlton to come to her rescue, but he only surveyed her quizzically.

The oration came. "My dear, I'm sure you don't realize to what extent you are penalizing your whole family, your whole homelife, by doing for this small stranger you have taken in."

"Stranger! I haven't taken in a stranger. We're keeping a little boy who happens to be the son of our best friends." *Oh, dear, she mustn't screech so.*

"It was only to be expected that you should help out for a few days, maybe a week, when tragedy struck. But a son is still the responsibility of his father. Hasn't

168

Joe Collins made any arrangements for him? Is he utterly indifferent to the strain he's imposing on you and yours?"

"Look, Uncle Matthew, I promised Kay—the very last time I saw her when she was heartsick with worry —that I'd see that Jodey—" *There went her voice hitting high decibels again.*

"My dear child, don't you know that promises to the dead are not binding either legally or morally? Not when they conflict with the well-being of the living."

"I know one thing. You legal-minded Buells can always twist anything into whatever you want. You'd think I'd learn that it's a waste of breath to argue—" She was screaming chokily, but she couldn't stop. She screamed even louder, "Maybe it would be legally and morally right just to open the door and kick him out. Is that what you want me—to—to—"

The close-to-the-surface tears came with a rush. She groped for a high stool, sat on it, and buried her face in her hands. She didn't lift it while Carlton ushered his uncle out. Or while he phoned his grateful client and voiced regrets over not being able to meet him that evening at the Rainbow Club. His wife had made other plans, he said.

Beany fumbled for a tissue, blew her nose, and said sudsily, "So I committed the unpardonable sin of not having ice for his lordship's drink! Why didn't you stop that long-play record instead of just standing there?"

Carlton chuckled. "Even if the Irish in you is spoiling for a scrap, I won't fight. I used up all my fight in court. Is this unsavory-looking something in the dish on top of the teakettle for Thumper or for human consumption?"

She couldn't help laughing. "If it ever thaws, it'll be breaded cutlets for dinner."

"Not tonight, it won't. I still insist on celebrating. If we can't go out to a party, we'll bring a reasonable facsimile in. Mary Liz, Mister, Jodey, listen. You get to choose between pizza and fried chicken. All in favor of pizza, raise your hands."

Three small hands went up promptly—four, counting Mary Liz's two. "Fried chicken?" The same number of hands went up.

"The ayes have it," he announced, and winked at Beany. "Pizza, it is. And you, Cutty Sark, will have nothing to do but soak in a bathtub until it arrives."

❧ 17 ❧

Beany was in the back yard the next noontime, shaking out a rosebud pillowcase to hang on the clothesline, when Joe Collins came through the side gate, calling out, "Anybody home?"

Jodey wasn't here, she told him. McNally had come over and taken him and his jug home with her. The two small Buells had gone with their father to see the Bombshells practice. "But I—honestly, Joe—if it were the Second Coming, I'd be either hanging up or taking down clothes."

He gave her an anxious look. "Do you feel better today?"

"I feel fine." He continued to survey her so concernedly that she asked, "Shouldn't I? You didn't expect to find me in a decline, did you?"

"Your Uncle Matthew said—I mean, he sounded like you'd just about cracked up."

She stared at him an incomprehensive moment. "Uncle Matthew told you that? Just when did he pass out that interesting information about me?"

"He phoned me at the rooming house last night. By dog, Beany, I never meant to impose on you so much or so long."

Beany said slowly, "Did he tell you you were imposing on me? And I suppose he stressed how I was neglecting my husband and children—and dear old Uncle Matthew—because of Jodey?"

"Well—yes. He said you weren't able to go out with Carl. I didn't realize how hard it was for you to get a baby-sitter for Jodey. I know he used to be hell on wheels with some people. Gosh, Beany, it's just that I've been working so hard, so's to get on top of my debts that I—"

"Uncle Matthew could try minding his own business," she ground out.

"I'm sure he meant well."

"Oh, sure, sure," she mocked. "He's like a father to Carl and me."

"I'm going to make a change," Joe said earnestly. "I've got to the point I can't bear that place I've got. I'm going to hunt around for a place where I can keep Jodey nights and weekends. You told me that Ander said I meant everything to Jodey—well, that kid means everything to me too." His voice thickened.

"Joe, you don't have to feel pushed by that meddlesome old fellow. It was just that yesterday was one of those days."

"I'll make it up to you someday, Beany, for all you've done." He glanced at his watch, and moved toward the gate. "Believe me, I never meant to impose on you so long or—like the old gent said—ride a free horse to death. Be seein' you." The gate clicked behind him.

Ride a free horse to death! What a cruel jibe to take at anyone who looked so work-mussed, so sagging and driven as Joe had when he hesitated at the gate. The gall of Uncle Matthew. Her anger lifted to the boiling point. She shook out the rosebud pillowcase so vehemently that it snapped like a whip.

The gate clicked again. It was Carlton, and he was whistling softly as though he still felt on top of the world. He explained to Beany that her one-time baby-sitter across the street had waylaid Mister and Mary Liz to show them the new pups that had just arrived last evening. And he had to leave right away to drive Uncle Matthew's wife to the airport.

"Can you imagine it, Beany, this is the third time Aunt Ruth has gone trekking off to Mexico this year?"

"Yes, I can imagine it," she snapped. "Is Uncle Matthew going to the airport with you?"

"Oh, sure, he has to see her off. Want to come too?"

"I certainly do. There's something I want to tell him—and the sooner the better."

He looked closely at her. Her lips were tight, her eyes blazing. "Like what?" he asked.

"Like when I married you, I didn't take any vows about having Uncle Matthew meddling in my life, or my having to kowtow to him—'Yes, Uncle Matthew. Sit here, Uncle Matthew—' until death us do part."

Carlton was slow to anger. A remnant of smile was still on his lips as he asked, "What's all this about anyway?"

"It's about Uncle Matthew taking it on himself to tell Joe Collins I'm teetering on the edge of a breakdown—probably mental as well as physical—all because there wasn't any ice for his Scotch last—"

"If he did take it on himself, it wasn't because there wasn't any ice, but because you were having the screaming meemies."

That remark added fuel to her flame. "Pardon me," she said in a mimicking voice, "for thinking you might possibly side with your wife against his Holiness."

"Don't talk foolish. It's not a question of siding with or against anyone."

"Oh, yes, it is. You agree with him about Jodey. You may even have put him up to—"

"Stop right there. Have I ever begrudged Jodey anything? I've said he's too much for you. I worry about it. And I'm telling you now that he—and the extra work and worry—are turning you into a fishwife. I have to leave." He reached for the knob on the French door.

"Wait. You've forgotten something." It was her mimicking voice again. "You forgot to remind me of how Uncle Matthew let us have his mountain cabin to honeymoon in. And even stocked the refrigerator for us."

She saw the muscles in his jaw tighten, and a small inner voice warned, You've been married to him four years, and you know by now that he won't yell back, but he'll turn stubborn as a mule. Yes, she knew it, but her anger drove her on.

"Oh, and you forgot to remind me that he let you

work in his office all the time you were getting your degree. If I promise to genuflect, can't I go to the airport with you and Uncle Matthew?"

He said coldly, "Yell just a little louder so the people at the end of the block can hear you," and went into the house. He didn't slam the door. She wished, somehow, he had.

She was still holding the rosebud pillowcase. Her fingers shook so that she had to try again and again to pin it to the line. . . . The woman across the street, where the Buell two now were, used to tell about the frequent rows she and her husband had. "He's the explosive kind." She would laugh and add, "But he'll come home to dinner with a box of candy or some flowers."

Carlton wasn't the explosive kind. Neither was he the kind to appease his wife with candy or flowers. . . .

In fact, he didn't come home for dinner that evening, but phoned to say briefly that he had been asked to keep the box scores on the games at the new lighted field. The chasm between them widened.

It widened still more as the days passed. You wouldn't think two people, who loved each other, could eat at the same table, sleep in the same bed, and still act with the chill courtesy of strangers. Two people *could* when each, wrapped in stubbornness and pride, waited for the other to make the first overture.

Uncle Matthew stopped as usual. Beany didn't berate him or even act cool toward him. On the contrary, she bent over backward to prove to him, as well as to Carlton, that caring for a little boy named Jodey was nothing at all. No matter how worrisome the day, she saw to it that she had showered and freshened up, and picked the house up, for the arrival of her Two Enemies. Often when she heard the car outside, she raced about to flatten the skittery scatter rugs and warn the three children, "Don't you dare muss them up."

Uncle Matthew's drink never lacked for ice cubes. One evening she provided a dish consisting of different bite-sized breakfast foods and peanuts all heated in the oven with butter, which was known on Laurel Lane as "munchers." This she passed to Uncle Matthew as though she had all the time in the world to spend on life's little niceties.

But she moved through her days with a stone in her chest. The children talked ecstatically about the new pups across the street, and she answered, "For goodness sake," without knowing what they said.

The second week of the cold war, Carlton drove a hundred and ten miles to a town to investigate a case. By now the stone in Beany's chest was the size of a boulder. By now her very hand hungered for the feel of Carlton's warm, firm clasp. She even muttered as she dressed Mary Liz, "I was the one that pounced on him and said every hateful thing I could think of. When he comes home, I'll tell him I didn't mean a word of it."

She would have his favorite foods—pot roast and Dutch apple pie—as a peace offering, too. She paid Ditso for an hour of lounging on the glider, drinking three bottles of Bartell's "Cherry Chill" and finishing off a can of peanuts, while she made a special trip to the supermarket for the roast and another to a vegetable stand for tart green apples.

But in the late afternoon, just when she was listening for the crunch of a car in their driveway, the phone rang. It was Connie, secretary at the Buell and Buell office, who said, "That man of yours just called, Beany. He wants me to look up some data for him and call him back. And he asked me to phone you, and tell you he'll be staying all night. Don't ask me why, because it sounds as though he's done all the damage he can there."

All Beany's excited anticipation turned rancid. *I can tell you why. Because it'll be a treat for him to be away from the fishwife he's married to. He even had you call me because he didn't want to hear my voice.*

"Any message?" Connie asked. "I have to call him back with his info."

The Irish side of Beany couldn't decide whether to say something that would hurt Carlton or to burst into tears. She did both. "Tell him I'm glad he's not coming home, Connie. Because I'm going out with some friends." And when the telephone was in place, she sat and sobbed in both anger and heartache while the pot roast sizzled brownly in the Dutch oven.

ᘒ 18 ᘒ

On Colorado Day, which was the first of August, the station wagon from Big Basin stopped at the Buell curb. Over the side of the attached trailer, Sir Echo's white-splashed face looked out.

Mary Fred was a picture in her matador outfit of turquoise velvet. Silver fringe trimmed the snug pants and the vest, and her wide hat and boots were cream-colored to match the ruffled shirt. So glowing, so happy, so bouncy, Beany thought wistfully. And I'm so drab, so miserable, and so not-a-bounce-in-a-carload.

Again Ander had to hold up a host of children to view and touch the palomino. But Jodey shook his head when Ander reached for him. "Horses are so big," he demurred.

"Look at Sir Echo smirk," Mary Fred said. "He knows he's going to be in a show, and he can't wait to show off."

"Ditto for my ever-loving wife," Ander said.

She laughed in delight. "We're a couple of hams,

aren't we, Echo? So everybody load in and come over to the stadium to see us do our fancy figures. And then let's all stuff ourselves with hot dogs and pop to last till Carl's cookout supper."

Mister and Mary Liz were all jumpy enthusiasm about going. "How about you, soldier?" Ander asked Jodey.

He, looking extremely dubious, backed into Beany. Because of her trying to prove to Carlton that Jodey required no special handling, she said heartily, "Sure, Jodey wants to see the show. I'm the one that can live without horses. Mary Fred used to say I was allergic to them. Go wash up, Jodey."

When he was out of earshot, she said, again for Carlton's benefit, "Do you notice how much better he is, Ander? He doesn't run away now. And he's perfectly contented when he's *making* something. McNally has got him painting little cans—first you stick little shell macaronis on them—to make pencil holders. Anybody want a pencil holder?"

"You and McNally have done wonders with him, Beany. Has the little fellow laughed yet?"

"No, not yet."

Ander had brought steaks from their ranch freezer and sweet corn from a vegetable stand along the road. They had to wait while Carlton put the steaks in a marinade and the corn in salt water, so that he could roast it, cowboy style, in its own husks over the coals. Carlton, who was a complete loss in a kitchen, excelled in outdoor cooking.

The Palomino Parade got under way with the usual

flag raising, the playing of the national anthem, and the Mayor, smiling and bowing to the crowd, as he was driven past the stand in a convertible.

"When are the horses going to dance?" Mister kept asking.

"They trot and gallop around first," Ander told him.

And so they did. Ander and Carlton took Mister and Mary Liz down to an unoccupied box overlooking the field so they could get a close-up of Mary Fred as she whisked by on Sir Echo. "Jodey and I will stay here," Beany said.

Yes, Jodey was better. He didn't get frightened until the show was well along, and the crowd and cheering increased, and when young people began leaping from one tier of seats to another. "Are they going to hurt us?" he asked.

"Goodness no, Jodey."

But he kept pressing closer to her, until his face was buried in her shoulder. "Look, Jodey, the horses are spelling C-O-L-O-R-A-D-O. Isn't it pretty?"

"Yes, but I don't like it." He wouldn't look up.

The riders were lining up for the Virginia reel when his desperate fingers plucked at her. "Mrs. Mother, I want to go home."

"Okay, Jodey, hold tight to my hand, and we'll go."

They picked their way down to the front of the grandstand where she could call out to Carlton and Ander, "I've had enough cavorting horses for now. Jodey and I are going on home."

She waved aside Mister's, "Don't you want to see

the horses dance?" and Ander's offer to drive her home. "No. No, it isn't far. You folks stay and watch the show."

She saw Carlton's eyes rest on the cringing little boy. She didn't fool him as to which one of them had had enough of cavorting horses.

The crowds and cheering were well behind them before Jodey's face lost its pinched look. "Maybe Dad will be home when we get there," he said.

They didn't walk the whole way home. A neighbor came by and gave them a lift when they had gone three blocks.

It was late afternoon before the sun dropped low enough in the west for the patio to be shaded. The station wagon and occupants had returned, hot and tired, an hour before. They had been delayed by picture taking, by the general jam of unsaddling horses and loading them into trailers.

The two small Buells were napping, but Jodey was waiting for his father. Mary Fred had showered and changed into a cool summery dress, and she answered Carlton's, "Aren't you pretty fancy for a cookout?" with, "But right after the cookout, we're going to a pretty fancy party. The Shriners are having a reception at the Hilton for all the riders in the show."

When the phone rang Mary Fred, the closest to it, picked it up. She put it down, and called to Jodey who was watching out the kitchen window. "That was your dad, Jodey, and he won't be along for a little while. He's off work, and either he's showered or he's about to. And he says he has to find a store that's open to buy wieners. He'll have one more stop to make, and then he'll be by to take you to a wiener roast."

"What's a wiener roast?"

Ander told him, "That's where you put wieners on a long fork or stick and hold them over the fire. Not close enough to burn—and you keep turning them around and around until the skin blisters and sizzles and pops." He was very graphic with his illustrative sounds. "A pointed stick is better than a fork. When I was about your age, I used to cut myself a crotched stick like this"—he held up two fingers in the shape of a V—"so I could roast two wieners at the same time."

Jodey said raptly, "I'd like to do two at a time, too."

"Well, sir, we'll just get you a good wiener-roasting stick. The trees in this yard are too new. But we can walk down to where the bridge crosses that little creek a few blocks away. There's a big willow there. We'll have time before your dad comes. Here, you can carry my cutting knife."

Beany watched the little blond boy and Ander set out.

Carlton donned his chef's apron and started the fire in the grill. Mary Fred, relaxed full-length on the outdoor chaise, made it look like an advertisement for lawn furniture. Beany was covering the weathered top of their picnic table with the red-checked cloth, when she heard the front screen door open and close, and Joe Collins's loud, "Anybody home?"

"Come on out, Joe," Carlton called, and Beany addressed the blue sweater she saw through the screen of the French doors, "We didn't think you'd get here so soon, and Ander took Jodey to cut himself a wiener-roasting stick."

Joe's easy laugh also came through the screen, "Didn't take me long. I found an open grocery right around the corner." He wasn't alone. He pushed open the screen door, and stood back for a young woman to precede him, saying over her shoulder as she did, "I think you all know Vonnie—Yvonne Plettner."

Her sandals clack-clacked down the two flat steps and onto the brick floor. She was holding the strings of three balloons, blown up to the size of basketballs.

For a moment there was an unbelieving silence. With Carlton holding the can of etherish-smelling starter fluid, with Beany smoothing a corner of red-checked cloth, and Mary Fred sitting up straight on the chaise. Yvonne said, "Oh, yes, I met you all at Kay's funeral, but then everyone was so heartbroken we hardly remember whom we met and whom we didn't."

You weren't heartbroken, Beany thought viciously. She couldn't say why the studied perfection of Yvonne's appearance irritated her so. Today she wore maroon slacks and a bulky coral sweater. And—wouldn't you know!—her lipstick *and* the polish on her fingernails and toenails were the same shade of dusty coral.

Joe was saying, "I believe I've got a deal worked out for Jodey so I can take the load off you folks, Beany and Carl. Vonnie called me night before last and asked me to come to her apartment and—"

The girl put in swiftly, "I'm moving. I'm just not the apartment type, and I'm going to live with these friends of mine, Betty Lou and Dick—I think I told you before that they came from Peachtree, too—and while I was packing, I came across a whole raft of high-school pictures that I thought Joe might like to have, because Kay was in a lot of them."

School pictures this time, instead of cupcakes. No, indeedee, you certainly don't let any grass grow under your prancy little feet with their coral polish.

"And Joe got to telling me how he was up a stump about little Jodey," Yvonne went on. "Right away, I thought of Betty Lou, and how she's already tied down with her two little girls. And they've bought this place out toward the airport with a big fenced-in yard. So I just picked up the phone and told Betty Lou the whole deal, and she said yes, she'd like to board a little boy. I think they've bit off more than they can chew in buying the place, between you and I and the gatepost."

Beany started to wink at Carlton over her preening use of the ungrammatical "between you and I" before she remembered that she and her husband weren't on winking terms.

Joe said, "Now that I'm getting my debts whittled down, I can pay—and be glad to—whatever Jodey's keep is worth. I told your Uncle Matthew I never meant to ride a free horse to death."

That could still rankle Beany.

Yvonne had more explaining to justify her being here with Joe. "I've been moving out of my apartment in bits and pieces—you know, taking a load out in my car every evening. So Betty Lou and Dick and I had already planned on this wiener roast in their back yard. Then Betty Lou asked Joe to come and bring Jodey, and that way everybody can get acquainted."

Strange, how tongue-tied everyone was except Yvonne, with Joe filling in now and then. But Yvonne, quite undaunted, went on, "I'm just not an apartment-house gal. I'll be a lot happier out there with Dick and Betty Lou. Gracious, I'm used to washing clothes and hanging them out on a line—not on hangers in a bath-room. And I love to cook." She laughed a pleased-with-herself laugh, "I guess I'm just an old hausfrau at heart."

Beany's very soul went chill. She could almost hear Yvonne on the phone: "Joe, I've fried two huge skillets of chicken, and we need someone to help eat it." All those neat little traps! And Joe, the naïve, the trusting, would bumble right into them.

Carlton spoke for the first time, "You'll have to see how Jodey hits it off with all those folks first, Joe."

Before he could answer, a commotion in the house announced Ander's and Jodey's return. Jodey had evidently seen his father's car in front of the house, for he was the first to come leaping through the door and down the steps to the patio.

❦ 19 ❧

Jodey was holding aloft his crotched stick, and crying out, "Look, Dad. Lookit how sharp the points are. I can put one wiener on this one, and another on this one." He had eyes for no one but his father. "And you hold it about this far from the fire, because you have to watch and not burn—"

Yvonne stepped up to him all smiles. "I brought you something, Jodey. I know how little boys like balloons." (The syrupy, talking-down voice.) "So you take the one you like best, and give the other two to your little friends here. Your father said he bet you'd like the red one."

Jodey didn't answer. He didn't move. All the happy radiance drained from his face. And into his eyes, which never lifted from Yvonne's face to the swaying balloons, came the dark cloud of fear. He backed up, until he was pressed hard against his father. Yvonne came closer, and held out the string of the red balloon to him. "Here you are, little man."

"No. No." The terror in his strangled scream

brought goose pimples to Beany's arms. Jodie pressed even tighter between his father's legs.

Joe bent down and took his arm. "I'm ashamed of you, son. Say thank you to Vonnie—Miss Plettner—for bringing you a present. She's known you since you were knee-high." He stepped back, robbing Jodey of the shelter of his legs. "Come on now, buckaroo, we're going to a picnic."

"No, no. Not with *her*. I don't want to go."

"What kind of talk is that. You'll have fun. Come on—"

The little boy wrenched himself from his father's grasp. He dodged past Carlton and the smoking grill. He sidestepped Beany, who involuntarily reached out for him. He was down the length of yard, and wedged out of sight between incinerator and fence under the low-hanging spirea bushes before anyone could draw a long breath.

The little rabbit again, bolting for cover.

Beany happened to glance at Yvonne. Her eyes, like all the others, were turned in the direction Jodey had taken and rested on the still quivering bushes. In that instant, and before she had time to veil them, Beany saw pure hate in them. Beany's goose pimples prickled again.

Joe Collins took an indecisive step toward the hiding place. "I'll crawl in after him. Once we get on our way, I'm sure he'll be all right."

Ander Erhart spoke sharply, "No, Joe, no. That would be the worst thing you could do."

"I don't know why he'd carry on like that," Joe

worried. "Beany and I were just talking the other day about how much better adjusted he's been lately."

"He is better," Ander said. "That's why it would be disastrous to have a setback now."

Joe stooped and picked up the crotched stick Jodey had dropped in his headlong flight. He touched its sharp points carefully, mournfully.

"He smoothed it and sharpened the points himself," Ander said. And Beany put in, "He likes to make things. Every time he comes home from McNally's he brings something he's made."

"I know." Joe turned to Yvonne. "You ought to see the little job he made out of one of those small orange-juice cans for me to keep pencils in."

Yvonne tied the balloon strings to the back of the glider. She said, "Joe, if you can't do anything about him hiding down there, I think we ought to go. Betty Lou and Dick and the children will be waiting for us. They can't very well have a wiener roast until you get there with the wieners. And I'm bringing the dessert."

Ah, more of those pink, pink cupcakes, no doubt.

"Yeah, I guess we'd better," Joe agreed unhappily.

"Come back as soon as you can, Joe," Beany urged. "Remember the day of Kay's funeral when he hid down there and how you were the only one he'd come out for?"

"I sure will, Beany."

The two left.

Neither Beany nor Carlton nor Ander could persuade Jodey to leave his hiding place. *"She* might come back," was his small-voiced answer.

Mary Liz, too, bent her small self double to catch a glimpse of the blond head under the sheltering branches. "Cob on the corn, Jodey. You come."

"After a while, I will," he promised.

The whole event cast a pall over their enjoyment of steaks and Carlton's specially roasted corn. Beany even felt spiteful relief when the last of the balloons popped. Mary Fred went inside to run a comb through her hair, put on lipstick and a dab of perfume. She came back to the patio to say, "Spruce yourself up a bit, Ander, and let's go on to the Shrine party."

"Not yet, Mary Fred. I'd like to talk to Joe when he comes."

He came, concerned and apologetic. It had been hard to get away from the folks out there. It had also been hard for him to explain Jodey's behavior. "I'm glad you waited, Ander. Those folks seemed to think that Jodey was just throwing a tantrum because he was jealous of Vonnie going with us. They seemed to think that none of us are tough enough with the kid."

Ander said wryly, "You saw the shape Jodey was in from the folks in Peachtree being tough—paddling him and roping him to a clothesline. It's easy to jump to the obvious conclusion—that he was jealous of your taking someone else. It's easy for the average person to see that a child on crutches isn't up to doing what other children do. But this average person can't see that a child can be crippled emotionally."

"I still can't figure out why he carried on so when he saw Vonnie," Joe muttered.

It was all Beany could do to keep from shouting:

She hated Kay. She said Jodey was a monster. She was at the hospital when Jodey was there. Maybe she was the *somebody* who hurt him.

Ander's mind must have been running somewhat parallel to hers. "I've been thinking about that, too, Joe. She's a nurse. Was she in training at the Peachtree hospital when Jodey was there with his broken bone?"

Beany answered for him, "Yes, she was there."

Ander thought aloud, "Evidently the poor little codger somehow connects her with the bad time he had at the hospital, and later on in Peachtree. She's part of his subconscious fear and mistrust. He just needs extra doses of what social workers call TLC—tender loving care—to work out of it."

Joe walked down to the bushes and squatted down, "Come on, buckaroo. There're still enough coals for you to toast your wieners. I brought some home for you."

"Is *she* still there?"

"No one's here but the family. Here, give me your hand."

Jodey came, dragging back while he looked over each person there on the patio. Carlton turned on the outdoor light so that he could feel reassured. Jodey's eyes sought his father's. "Will she come back?"

"No, she won't come back. Don't you worry."

But Beany worried. Not about Yvonne coming back to Laurel Lane, but about Joe's going out to that house near the airport to a meal Yvonne cooked on her day off.

Mary Fred had interrupted Ander's conversation with Joe and Beany on the patio. "As long as we missed the reception, we ought to start home so Sir Echo can stretch his cramped legs."

Now they were taking the road north to Big Basin and the Erhart ranch. Mary Fred spoke edgily. "It's getting to be a pattern—Jodey Collins spoiling every trip we make to Denver. I needn't have bothered taking along a dress to wear to the party."

This time Ander didn't say he was sorry about her upset plans. He roused to ask, "Did you have a feeling of mistrust for that Yvonne that Joe brought out?"

"I had a definite feeling that she's got her hooks out for Joe."

"Did you sense the awful animosity between her and Jodey?"

"Yes, I did." Mary Fred laughed ruefully. "And so did I sense the animosity between Beany and Carl. They didn't speak to each other except when they had to, and then you could knock icicles off their words. But what can you expect with an emotional Beany, who thinks with her pulse beats, and a logical—but darn stubborn—fellow like Carl?"

Ander didn't answer that, but sighed, "If only Joe hadn't brought that prancy little Yvonne out. Just when Jodey was coming out from under his dark cloud. He was like any enthusiastic kid when we got his wiener-roasting stick. Once I even thought he was going to laugh."

Mary Fred said, and there was fright in her voice,

"Are you thinking you'd like to take him to live with us—if you didn't have an unsympathetic wife?"

He skipped the unsympathetic-wife part and answered promptly, "No. I thought about it once. I even talked about it to Nels at Colorado General, and he said no, that it would be catastrophic for Jodey. Because it would disrupt his father relationship which is Jodey's buckler and shield. He has to have that my-dad's-bigger'n-you to cling to."

Silence fell and lengthened. The miles ticked off. Mary Fred was so close to him that their shoulders touched, and yet she could feel that he was far, far away from her.

Only Beany and Carlton moved about the quiet house on Laurel Lane. Joe left after putting Jodey to bed. Mister and Mary Liz were fast asleep.

Beany put the last dish away in the cupboard, and went out to set the patio to rights. Carlton had left the embers in the grill to burn themselves out. He was inside, stacking heavy law books on the dining-room table and pulling it closer to the wall lamp.

Mister had asked him, "Are you going to hunt a precedent again?" and when his father nodded, he pursued, "What will you do with it when you catch it?"

"I'll get a tight hold on its neck and take it to court with me tomorrow," Carlton told him. Again there had been no sharing wink between him and Beany.

She was suddenly too heavy of heart and limb to take another step. She dropped down on the glider.

Today had been the despairing climax of that whole despairing question, *Who'll look after Jodey?*

She scrunched lower on the glider to be out of the light streaming out through the French doors. She lay, watching the windows go dark in the houses behind them, and envied the couples who, with no chill formality, were asking each other if the dog was in and were the tricycles still out on the pavement.

The snick-snick of the swing grew slower, fainter. Her last waking thought was a troubled prayer she sent upward, "What are we going to do?". . .

She came out of her heavy sleep slowly. She must have slept an hour—maybe more—for there was that dark, late-at-night stillness all about her. Not even a cricket chirped, or a dog barked in the distance. She lifted herself onto her elbow.

She couldn't believe it. She had gone to sleep muddled and weary, and she wakened serene and refreshed.

The light from the open door was blocked by someone standing in the doorway. Carlton must have finished his hunt for a precedent. He came down the steps. "You'd better not lie here without something over you. The nights turn cool." The icicles Mary Fred had mentioned hung from every word.

She looked up at him and said wonderingly, "Uncle Matthew was right, Carl. I *have* sacrificed all of you for Jodey. It's so clear now. I've snapped at Mister and Mary Liz—of course, Mary Liz was born under a bright star, and it would take more than that to throw her. But Mister is more sensitive—"

Carlton covered a sleepy yawn.

Beany hurried on, "And you were right when you said it was too much for me. Do you know why it was? Because I wasn't big enough. I thought all I needed was stronger patience and coping muscles, but that wasn't enough. I didn't have enough love to go around. You know that quote—something about even if you have faith to move mountains, and have not charity— Only Andy Kern told me once that it should read *love* instead of charity—"

"Charity is from the Latin *cara,* meaning love," he said, and yawned again.

Automatically she pulled her feet up until her knees were almost touching her chin to make room for him in the glider. Automatically he sat down. He said, and there was despair in his voice, "Joe's plans for Jodey with those folks certainly came to a big fat zero. But I still think it's too much for you."

"It'll be different now. I feel—strong. It's like a miracle—like maybe an angel came along and re-charged my batteries while I was asleep." He didn't answer. Even his silence was skeptical. She didn't wonder. She, the screaming fishwife, was a fine one to talk about love and angels. "Let me have another chance at taking care of Jodey, Carl."

"Please, Beany, let's not talk about it now." The very weariness in his voice said for him, "He's been the bone of contention we've bickered and quarreled over, but now I'm too tired."

The very weariness under his words and the weariness of his slumped figure sent a rush of tenderness through her. "Carl, you ought to go up in the mountains and tramp around and fish. You need a vacation."

"It wouldn't be a vacation unless you and the little fellows were along."

Just as involuntarily as she had made room for him on the glider, she reached out to him. And, just as involuntarily as he had taken the space she offered, he took her hand and his, firm and warm, closed over it.

The world was right again. A time for words, a time for keeping still. So she didn't say, "Husbands need TLC—meaning tender, loving care—too, and I've certainly short-changed you." But she moved closer to him. He pulled their clasped hands up and held hers against his cheek. It was almost as though he said, "Together we can work it out—somehow."

They sat on in the velvety darkness under the stars. So still. Only the glider chirp-chirped gently, and the grill gave out a final breath of charcoal smoke like a whiff of incense. A brief and beautiful caesura out of the hurry-scurry of their days.

It was well past midnight when McNally dragged up the stone steps of the darkened house on Hawthorne and let herself in the heavy carved door. Her Colorado Day schedule had called for her working at the Buckeye from eight in the morning until four in the afternoon. But Jen, her relief, had phoned from a nearby town that she and her boy friend were stuck with a leaky radiator. McNally was not surprised because the boy friend's hobby was antique cars. "I'll be there just as soon as I can," Jen promised.

In the hall, dimly lighted by the globe Winged Mercury held aloft, McNally kicked off shoes, pulled off stockings, and wriggled red and swollen feet.

Alice Henderson appeared at the head of the stairs, a shadowy figure but with a full-bodied voice of indignation, "Do you mean to tell me that snide little Jen never showed up at all?" Without waiting for the answer which was obvious, she added, "Did you see the message I left there on the phone stand?"

McNally's very fatigue made her light-headed and somehow giddy. "No. My public will have to wait till morning."

"The message was to tell you Maria Godwin—you know, of the Maria Godwin School—phoned. Twice. The first time, I told her I expected you back any time. She called again—and we talked."

I'll bet you did. I'll bet you told her about my being jilted and the taxes being overdue, and that you think it's a sin for me to be wasting my talents at the Buckeye Bar and Grill.

Alice Henderson went on, "Mrs. Godwin wants you to be one of her teachers. She said she'd never had one that fitted in so well down there or that the children were so happy with."

McNally said irrelevantly, "Did you know that a boy at school, named Andy Kern, used to call me Apple-cheeks?"

And old Apple-cheeks McNally went down to that kindergarten school by the railroad tracks. It's no trick to hand out happiness to little children when you're

full and running over with it. What could I give them
now? If I tried to sing, my voice would creak.

"I told Mrs. Godwin you'd call her in the morning. You will, won't you?" the voice at the head of the stairs demanded.

McNally stood at the foot of them, holding her grubby white shoes, looking small and desolate and stubborn. "No, I won't call her. If she calls again, tell her I already have a job that keeps me pretty busy."

❧ 20 ❧

Beany had need of her "recharged batteries" in the days that followed. For Yvonne's appearance had brought to the fore again and re-emphasized Jodey's somebody's-going-to-hurt-me fears.

Beany told Ander about it when he phoned a few days later from Big Basin to ask about him. "The poor kid won't come out of his room in the morning until I tell him there's no one but *us* in the house. He doesn't go running out to the truck when Joe stops. He waits at the door to be sure *she* isn't with him."

The one place Jodey seemed to feel sure of safety was at McNally's. He waited three anxious days for her to change to the late four to midnight shift and for Beany to drive him to Hawthorne Street. Beany noted with a slight tinge of jealousy, what relaxed comfort he drew when the heavy door closed behind him.

But Beany, too, found solace in her visits there. She missed Miggs now in Texas. She missed and grieved over Kay. And why was Mary Fred so restless and discontented of late? "I seem to need a friend to confess or explode to," Beany had told McNally once.

So this morning, while Jodey guided the vacuum and Mister and Mary Liz climbed up the stairs and bumped down them, Beany confessed her vitriolic outburst about Uncle Matthew's meddling and exploded over Yvonne's appearance that had sent Jodey racing for the spirea bushes.

For once McNally wasn't mixing paint, making over curtains, or struggling with a slipcover. She sat with her hands lax. Beany ended, "Listen to me, running on and on like Tennyson's brook. Now tell me about you."

McNally shrugged. "Nothing to tell, except that I had an estimate on weatherproofing the sleeping porch upstairs, and it's more than I can afford. Alice—you remember Mrs. Henderson?—has it all figured that we could rent it and the bedroom it opens off of as a two-room suite. She doesn't like to have any empty rooms in the house."

But about the empty rooms in her heart, McNally said nothing.

Alice Henderson did. She was starting for work that day when Beany, leaving Jodey behind with McNally, carried Mary Liz down the stone steps. Mister disdained even her guiding hand.

Alice Henderson walked to Beany's car with her. "Did Linda—McNally, as you call her—tell you that Maria Godwin wants her to come down there and teach? You've heard of the Maria Godwin School?"

"Oh, yes, I guess everyone has. Everyone quotes

her, 'Children and animals are more compatible when the animals are pat-able.' No, McNally didn't tell me. That's wonderful."

They had reached Beany's car. "She isn't going," the woman said. "She won't even answer Mrs. Godwin's call." A troubled pause, and then she said slowly, "I know how she suffered losing her mother and father, and that fellow she worshiped—all in only a few months. I know how it hurts her yet to see strangers in her mother's bedroom and to have to sell her father's desk to buy an apartment-sized icebox. Sometimes I wish she'd break down and cry—or get mad. I've tried every way to reach her. Maybe she'll listen to you, Mrs. Buell."

And maybe she won't.

On her way home, Beany stopped at the old Buell home on Barberry. The renters, now returned from their vacation, gladly gave her permission to search throughout basement and attic for a brown jug for Ditso. It was Mister who found one which, when dusted off, was almost a replica of the one that had crashed on the Buell patio.

Beany and the children went next door to the Malone home. Her father was not there, but Adair called a greeting to them from his study. She was sitting on the floor, and Beany knew that the great clutter of newspaper clippings, scissors, and tubes of paste meant that Adair was bringing a scrapbook, the size of a bread board, up to date with Martie Malone's columns.

Beany asked, "Remember that piece Dad did on

Maria Godwin's unusual kindergarten with the tomato plants and a monkey that scolded the kids about something—"

"For taking a bite out of an apple and throwing it away," Adair finished. "The piece is right here. I just glued it in. Careful—it's a double page with a tail I had to bend back. I went down with Martie when he interviewed her. Her husband and little boy died in a German prison camp. An amazing woman. She said she saw something of her own son in every child—no matter what color—down there."

Beany reread the article and looked at the almost too candid camera shot of a woman with untidy gray hair and weathered face. Then she gathered up her protesting two and the precious jug, and drove home stopping on the way at Ditso's where she heard not the grateful thanks she expected, but a muttered, "Not as good a fingerhold as the old one."

Later that afternoon, Beany waited outside for McNally to stop with Jodey. He, armed with a pail he had covered with wallpaper, raced inside to show it to Mary Liz. McNally was later than usual. She didn't get out of the car or turn off her motor. Beany had to talk to her through the let-down car window. And, because there was no time to lead up to it, she said earnestly, "McNally, please don't pass up that job at Maria Godwin's."

"So that gabby Alice told you!"

"Yes, and on my way home today, I read over Dad's piece about her and her school. And I couldn't help wondering if it couldn't be the answer for Jodey. He'll soon be five, McNally. If you were down there, he wouldn't be scared." McNally only stared resentfully at her, and Beany hurried on, "There was a picture of the wishing well, and the write-up said there were children who had never seen a radish or tulip grow, so Mrs. G. lets each youngster plant something—"

"A tomato plant," McNally broke in harshly. "Each one sets it out before school is out for the summer, and when they come back in the fall they harvest *their* tomatoes. I have to go."

Beany put a detaining hand on her arm. "And I loved Dad's quote about her taking children both from the slums and from rich homes, because she didn't want to deprive the wealthy ones." McNally looked straight ahead, and Beany hurried on, pitching her voice over the throbbing engine, "You're so wonderful with children. Look at what you've done for Jodey."

"That's because we have the same theme song, 'I've been hurt, and I'm afraid.' That's why we took to each other from the start." Her voice was gravelly. "You and your wondering about Jodey down there! He'd be scared out of his skin with all that riffraff. Besides, I'm a very good waitress—or didn't you know?"

Beany went on stubbornly, "I remember when we used to have coffee at the Student Union, and you'd talk about teaching small children—"

"Sure, sure. A child's mind like a rosebud unfolding," she mocked.

Beany said helplessly, "Alice Henderson said she couldn't understand why you kept on at the Buckeye instead of teaching, and, by gosh, McNally, neither can I."

The girl in the car reached out and turned off the chugging motor. She said with driven patience, "Maybe you won't understand this either, Beany. But last Thanksgiving when I turned away from the phone after talking to Phil's wife—and while I was still numb—I heard Mother fall. The car accident did something to her spine—don't ask me what, because four specialists couldn't figure it out. But sometimes she could walk, and then again she'd just drop. It was the same with her mind. Sometimes she'd be lucid enough and then—for instance, that day she was try- ing to get her fur coat out of the hall closet to go to a football game with Dad. Anyway I had her to care for. You know how a dentist blocks off the nerve when he's going to pull a tooth? I blocked off everything that had to do with Phil. I've managed, somehow, to keep it that way—because I know the minute the block goes, the pain will start."

Beany only stood silent, and ached for her.

"Go ahead, and tell me there's no use crying over spilt milk," McNally challenged. "Tell me there are more fish in the sea than have ever been caught. Re- member I never had the dates you and Kay did. I was little old chubby Apple-cheeks. For the four years of college, I never thought a thought that wasn't wrapped around Phil. Maybe you're still wondering, Why the Buckeye instead of the Godwin kindergarten? Because, goon, *he* always took me down and came after me, and

203

we'd sit on the edge of the wishing well, and he'd tease the monkey—I've got to go," she said with driven urgency, and turned on the motor.

The car gave a frantic leap forward as she stepped hard on the gas. *She couldn't get to the Buckeye fast enough. She couldn't get into that brown and yellow uniform soon enough, and take on the identity of a swift-moving automaton who asked, "What kind of beer?" and "Baked potato or French fries?" She could even sneer at herself: Jodey and his spirea bushes. Me and my Buckeye Bar and Grill.*

But she drove faster.

Summer seemed to be making its final demands before fall and school's opening. . . . Would Mrs. Buell bring a cake or pie to St. Mary's bake sale on Saturday? Yes, Mrs. Buell would. . . . "Beany, I know Thursday isn't your day to guard the pool at Mamie Eisenhower"—Beany's neighbor was referring to the small neighborhood park, named after the former First Lady—"but could you do it for me, because a whole flock of in-laws are descending on us?" . . . "Sure, Marge."

The Kincaids next door left their house key with Beany when they went on vacation. They'd appreciate it so much if she would feed, water, and clean the cage of their parakeet while they were gone. Beany had also to remember to keep Thumper shut up in Mister's room when it was time for their mail delivery, because of his violent dislike for the substitute mailman.

Then on a Sunday evening, Jodey's bracelet, with all

the bean-sized baseballs, basketballs, and footballs, disappeared. He was inconsolable. He accused Mister of taking it, and an outraged Mister retaliated by pulling the painted shell macaroni off the pencil holder Jodey had made for "Mrs. Mother." Nothing crunches quite so grittingly underfoot as a shell-shaped bit of pasta that has dried under a coating of gold spray.

Beany put off her Monday washing to hunt for it. She moved furniture, looked under couch pillows, and pulled every bed in the house apart. She emptied wastebaskets, piece by piece, and shook out the vacuum cleaner bag.

In the night she thought of the sandbox and the things she had found buried there. The next day she marked it off in fourths and sifted through every inch of it. She found her set of attached measuring spoons, one of Carlton's chess pieces, and an unidentified earring. But no bracelet known in Peachtree school circles as "the ball and chain."

It was mid-afternoon when Beany started the delayed washing. She found the bracelet in the butterfly pocket of Mary Liz's Sunday dress.

That evening, Beany was slumped down again on the glider on the dark patio. Carlton came out, and again she made room for him. "What are you doing out here all by your ownself, as Mister says?"

"I'm just sitting here, hoping for another miracle. Hoping that the same angel will pass this way again, and recharge my batteries."

⚜ 21 ⚜

Beany's date for acting as hostess at her book club luncheon fell on the Friday before Labor Day. It so happened that Dulcie was to entertain the Dames the day before that.

On Wednesday Dulcie came to the Buells' in the Trighorn pickup and asked, with a shade of embarrassment, if she could borrow Beany's love seat for her party. "Some of them are great on antiques, and I'll get it back in time for your booky friends to sit on."

Dulcie's wanting the once-scoffed-at love seat was surprise enough, but when she nodded toward Adair's painting of Barberry Street and asked, "Would you lend me that, too—just for the duration of the Dames?" Beany could scarcely believe her ears.

But Beany's heart went out to her. The only home Dulcie had ever known, between her father's meanderings from one mountain town to another and her marrying Trig, had been a ramshackle two rooms on which her carpenter father had started a cinder-block addition. After eight years, it still wasn't finished and, as Dulcie said, stuck out like a bruised thumb.

If Dulcie wanted the Dames to think her girlhood was spent in one of those three commodious houses with lawn and trees, Beany would aid and abet her.

Beany stood on a chair and lifted the picture from its hook (leaving a rectangle of virgin cream wall) and said as Dulcie took it, "There you are, toots. Take your choice—the one with the ruffles, or the hard-used one, or your mausoleum."

Dulcie gave her head a flip toss. "You never can tell. I just might be a judge's daughter by tomorrow."

Beany laughed in conspiratorial delight. "How about going whole hog and taking whatever Buell silver you need? It came from Carl's mother's side and—would you believe it!—it's initialed _L_ because she was a Lindsey."

"Made to order," Dulcie exulted. "The Dames have heard me say my name was Lungaarde before I was married." She drove home with the love seat, painting, salad forks, iced-tea spoons, and a beautiful old tea set, complete with "dreg bowl" for cold, leftover tea.

The Friday morning of the book club meeting, Adair came and took Mister and Mary Liz off Beany's hands for the day. McNally, again on the late shift, looked forward to having Jodey. "And don't worry about my bringing him back in the middle of the book review. I'll keep him until you phone that your last book clubber has left. I worked overtime for Jen at the Buckeye, so she will fill in for me until I get there."

Beany took Jodey over to Hawthorne Street before

stopping at a store for blanched almonds for her chicken salad. McNally came to the door with the morning paper in her hand. "Beany isn't the only one having a party today, Jodey. How'd you like to go to City Park to an at home for Charley Brown?"

"Charley Brown?"

"He's the baby elephant. The paper says he's been in seclusion in the elephant house with his mother, but today he'll be out in the yard between twelve and three to receive visitors. And while we're about it, we'll visit the monkeys. I've got a sack of peanuts for you to feed them."

Beany left them with their plans and went hurrying on. Dulcie might be waiting for her at home with the borrowed goods.

The book club members always met at one for what had started as a dessert luncheon but had grown into a fair-sized meal. (Beany's chicken salad was preceding a peach angel whip pie.)

What was keeping Dulcie? At half past eleven, Beany dialed her number. Dulcie, nervous and apologetic, answered with a long explanation. Yesterday at the party, one of the Dames had noticed her wall oven, installed by Trig. She had phoned early this morning to ask Dulcie if she could bring over her visiting uncle to see it. He was the handy type, and he thought he could copy Trig's in installing one for her.

"Gosh, Beany, she sounded as though they were starting right away, so I said sure, come ahead. I've been waiting and waiting. Just now I tried to phone her, but no answer. What can I do? I could leave the house open—it'd be safe enough—but then she'd see that the love seat and picture were gone. After all my blab-blabbing about them yesterday. This gal is the one that has the picture of her Maryland home and the trotters. Oh, here they come now. The minute they leave, I'll be right out. I can make it in twenty-five minutes this time of day."

Time went fast with Beany mixing salad, answering the phone to tell one member that yes, her house guest would be more than welcome, and another that no, she wouldn't need ice cubes. She whipped cream for the peach pie. She was amazed to see, when she turned to glance at the clock, that it was a quarter to one. Her book clubbers were due in fifteen minutes.

She dialed Dulcie's number, and heard it buzz four times—five— That must mean that Dulcie was on her way over. And then the receiver was lifted, and Dulcie said a breathless hello.

"It's Beany. Remember me? I'm the one who lent you some things that I happen to need for my own—"

Dulcie broke in on a choked sob, "They just—now —left. That slow-poky old geezer—he even called to me from the car—with more—questions. I kept try-ing—and trying—to get them out of—the house—"

One seldom heard the brash and cocky Dulcie break down and cry. Beany's anger melted away. "Well, don't feel bad, Dulcie. It's no life and death matter."

"But your love seat—and—the painting—and—"

209

"Mrs. Kincaid won't mind if I borrow a few chairs to fill in. I have to race over anyway to help myself to ice cubes. I've got another picture I'll put up."

"But what—what about forks—and spoons?"

This was harder to accept graciously, but Beany managed, "I can use my everyday stainless steel."

Dulcie was not much on voicing gratitude. She said, "That's swell of you not to be sore." And then, being Dulcie, she added, "But you don't have to worry about impressing people. Everybody knows who you Malones are, and the Buells, too."

The first carful of guests helped Beany carry over chairs and ice cubes from the Kincaids.

The whole meeting went off happily. Beany was asked for recipes for her chicken salad and peach angel whip pie. Their most serious member reviewed a biography of Count Leo Tolstoy. The less serious ones giggled and wisecracked over Tolstoy's preaching that women were sensual traps to be avoided when he himself made no effort to avoid them.

When the last car pulled away, Beany phoned McNally. Jodey answered, and she asked, "How did you like Charley Brown?"

A pause, and then, "When Miss McNally said he was a baby, I didn't think he would be so big."

"Even baby elephants are pretty big. Did you like the monkeys better? Did you feed them your peanuts?"

"No. Didn't you know there are *two* fences between people and the monkeys? There was one that kept looking at me and making faces at me and putting out his little-bitty thin hand, but I couldn't throw peanuts through two fences."

"Goodness, I forgot." That second wire fence was fairly new. Its installation allowed spectators to enjoy the monkeys' antics, yet prevented the tossing in of food, often indigestible to them.

"Miss McNally hurt her ankle. But it's nothing to worry about." Beany smiled at Jodey's apt quoting of McNally, and at his further quoting, "I am her legs."

McNally came to the phone, and Beany asked her about her ankle. "I twisted it getting out of the car. It's the same one that used to discombobble me once in a while when I was skating. So I'll just do what the doctor ordered then—bind it tight, and use it some but not too much. I'm having someone else take my place at the Buckeye for tonight."

"I'll ask Adair to swing by for Jodey when she brings our two home."

"Beany, I believe I'll keep him here tonight. He wants to stay and help me, and he's so disappointed by his trip to the park, and not getting within peanut-throwing distance of the monkeys. So I thought we'd work at making a papier-mâché one this evening, and see if that will satisfy him."

A strong wind came up at dawn. Through her sleep, Beany heard their milk box, empty bottles and all, blow over. Later, when they were breakfasting, the lightweight patio chairs went clattering across the brick floor to land in the sandbox.

Ordinarily, when Beany was hanging out her washing, she could hear the telephone's ring through the open French doors, but not this morning with the clothes snapping and crackling in the wind. Mister came running to tell her she had a call.

It was Joe Collins. She told him of Jodey's stay with McNally. "You know how wonderful she is with him."

Joe explained that today, with the anticipated heavy consumption of soft drinks over Labor Day, he'd be kept on the go until late. "But tomorrow, Beany, I'd like to stop in and see you and Carl. Something's just come up that I want to talk over with you, and ask you what you think. Will you be home tomorrow?"

"Yes, Carl's having a cookout again. Our two caught the wiener-roasting bug from Jodey. So you come too, Joe." Beany's curiosity overcame her. "Is everything all right on the job?"

"Couldn't be better. No, it's about my making a move— Remember my telling you I wanted to make a change, because this woman where I'm rooming is more than I can take with her constant bragging about her grandchildren. I'd rather explain it to you tomorrow."

It wasn't until Beany hung up that the awful thought struck her. Was this some more of Yvonne's sly conniving? Had she talked him into moving out with Betty Lou and Dick? Had she appealed to his loyalty to help out his fellow Peachtreeites? "Between you and I and the gatepost, Joe, your room rent would help on their house payments."

An uneasy Beany went out to take clothes off the

line before the wind did it for her. Mister summoned her again to the telephone. She knew who it was the minute she put the receiver to her ear and heard the vacuum cleaner rumbling in the background.

"How's the ankle today, McNally?"

"The ankle? It's about the same. I just have to humor it a little."

"Want me to come over after Jodey?"

"No-no, that's why I called. Let's wait—maybe I'll keep him another day." She sounded troubled and indecisive. "I don't like to bring him back when he's still so disappointed—"

"Oh, over the inaccessible monkeys? I tell you, both of you come over tomorrow for Carl's wiener roast in the back yard. Mary Fred and Ander will be down. And I asked Joe —Woops, there goes one of my sheets sailing through the air. We'll look for you and Jodey tomorrow then."

The crib-size sheet capsized on the hedge between the Buell and Kincaid yards.

✿ 22 ✿

The grayish papier-mâché substance clung to the dining-room rug in spite of all Jodey's vacuuming. McNally rubbed disgustedly at a spot with the toe of her tennis shoe. She might have saved herself all the mess and time of fashioning a replica of a monkey, because it had done nothing to lessen Jodey's little-boy grief over bringing back his sack of peanuts, instead of seeing his monkey friend crack and eat them.

"Did you ever shake a monkey's hand, Miss McNally?"

"Not hand, paw. No, I never craved to, but I knew a monkey that would shake hands with children." Now why had she said that? Now he would leave her no peace. She tried to dampen his interest with, "But sometimes he wouldn't shake hands at all. Sometimes this monkey—his name was Pedro—would stay up in the walnut tree and sulk and scold. Once he dropped a walnut on my head out of pure meanness."

"He did?" An almost smile quivered on his lips. "I

would like to have him drop a nut on my head. Could we go to see him, and could I take my peanuts and give them to him?"

"All right, we'll go." She said it in helpless anger. She was sick of Beany's nagging, sick of her own twinges of guilt. She would take Jodey down to the Maria Godwin School grounds. Even though school wasn't in session, there'd be sure to be a handful of small ruffians there—Maria Godwin never turned them away. Besides the temperamental Pedro, there'd be the donkey and perhaps a mongrel dog or cat. And if all that didn't make Jodey run for cover, Maria Godwin herself, with her direct way and foreign accent, would.

And then she could say to Beany, "You can stop wondering about the Godwin School being the answer for Jodey. He doesn't want any part of it. And you can stop telling me how to live my life, too."

"I'll take the peanuts," Jodey was saying.

"Yes, and one of the flowers that grow by the porch to drop in the wishing well. I've got something to drop in, too." With that same grim defiance of wanting to settle something for once and for all, she climbed the stairs to her room, reached into the lower drawer of her chifforobe and unclasped a fraternity pin from a red slipover.

Through the buffeting wind and with Jodey beside her, she drove down to the lower part of town and stopped outside of what, in early days, had been a bakery. The double gates in the shoulder-high fence were wide enough for a team and wagon to go through, and over them now was a sign, "M. Godwin. Kindergarten School." If only M. Godwin had gone on vacation before school's starting, and the gates were locked! That in itself would be McNally's answer.

They were not locked. This time she was the one who felt an inner trembling and the one who reached out for the little boy's hand and grasped it tight.

Inside the gates, the wind's impact was less. Its sweep was broken on one side by the school, née bakery, and on the other by a squarish brick building, once a Y.W.C.A. but now a warehouse for a box company.

These grounds were truly a kindergarten, or children's garden. A bed of onions, next to pansies. A tall walnut tree, accessible only to the monkey, and a spreading apple, accessible to all. The low sheds at the back had once housed the bakery carts and the horses that drew them. Doves now fringed their roofs, and the donkey looked boredly out. The wishing well, with its rock sides, had once been a watering trough.

Four children were in the garden. Two well-dressed boys were surveying the staked-up tomato plants, bearing red and green fruit. Two girls were gathering the windfall apples under the tree. One was a thin wisp of little girl with her fair hair matted and a bruise on one cheek; the other, a Negro, in a coat with sleeves that came down over her nimble hands, smiled gleefully at the visitors. "Hello, Miss McNally. I bet you don't remember me. I grew since you were here."

McNally waited for Jodey to press fearfully against her. He didn't. He was watching the two girls dropping apples in a supermarket sack, and when one asked, "Want one?" he said without shrinking, "No, I don't think so."

The door of the school opened, and Maria Godwin came out, carrying a bowl of oatmeal and milk. She smiled warmly at McNally in no surprise but as though she were expecting her. She set down the bowl for a gaunt calico cat that came running, and explained to McNally and Jodey, "Five kittens she has pulling at her to keep her hollow."

McNally had forgotten what an unorthodox dresser she was. The man's shirt she wore was half in, half out, of a full fiesta skirt, which dipped low on one side because of a hammer and no telling what else in the baggy pocket. Her one vanity was her small feet, and on those she wore lovely gray suede after-ski boots.

At sight of the Madonna face under the gray hair and those infinitely kind and understanding eyes, McNally's throat tightened. For the first time she felt an overwhelming and weary nostalgia for the girl she had been and the life she had led.

But she had left the decision to fate in the form of Jodey.

Maria Godwin bent down to him. "So you, little boy, have brought peanuts for that Pedro monkey. He is up in the tree over your yellow head. First you throw the flower in the wishing well and make a wish. Then you shake the sack, and soon you will see him peeking down, because he is greedy for nuts."

Again McNally waited for him to press tight against

her. He had never heard *is* pronounced *iss,* and *greedy* as *gritty* before.

But he only looked at the woman, absorbing the gentleness in her face. Dutifully he dropped the flower over the rock sides of the well. He shook his sack and peered upward at the branches of the tree, "I can see him peeking down," he whispered.

Yes, Alice Henderson must have told Mrs. Godwin a great many things that day she talked to her. For now she said, "You are Jodey, are you not? You wouldn't be afraid of anyone hurting you down here, would you?"

He brought his upturned head back in place. "No, I wouldn't be afraid. Did you see? The monkey came down another limb of the tree."

Maria Godwin turned to McNally, who still leaned against the well, her hand clenched. "Many people have been generous since that nice Mr. Malone wrote about us in the paper. A man's club sent us some desks. I would like you to advise about how best we should place them."

McNally nodded. "First—I have—something—to toss in the wishing well." She held her hand out over it and unclenched her fingers. The tiniest possible swish as a geometric-shaped bit of gold dropped beneath the wind-blown leaves and Jodey's flower.

That movement unblocked the nerve. The pain came throbbing through her. *For four years he told you he couldn't live without you. And in less than four months he was married to someone else.* She cowered under it. And then she slowly straightened and looked at Mrs.

Godwin, who was watching her, and sharing the hurt. McNally breathed aloud with shaky triumph, "But I can stand it—I can stand it."

Maria Godwin didn't quote any of the bromides. She said matter-of-factly, "Yes, my small one, even unbearable pain we can bear."

⚛ 23 ⚛

The wind was blowing in Wyoming, too, that Saturday before Labor Day. Each time a customer opened the door of the drugstore in Big Basin, the pasteboard sign, advertising a toothpaste that brightened while it whitened, toppled over. Each time Mary Fred Erhart, sitting at the fountain, would reach around and set it straight again. And then go back to watching out the window for the long gray car, which Ander drove so expertly, to come racing into town.

. . . Strange, how a telephone conversation with a person you have never laid eyes on can be as revealing as a lightning flash to a wayfarer lost at night. The sudden lifting of darkness discloses the landscape clearly, and shows the traveler how far off the road he has strayed. . . .

The phone call had come from Ander's friend, Dr. Nelson, in the Child Guidance Clinic in Denver. Would Mary Fred give Ander a message for him. Tell Ander he had come across a book by a German psychiatrist on the handling of the disturbed child. "It's right up the alley of what he and I were talking over about Jodey. Tell him I'll hold it here till he comes."

"I will, Dr. Nelson. We're planning on going to Denver tomorrow."

There had been a slight pause, and then the doctor, whom Ander described as a blunt Swede, asked, "Why didn't Ander go ahead and specialize in child psychiatry the way he planned? Out of all our class he was the one that had a savior complex about doing for these around-the-bend kids. He's still got it. I've been wondering what sidetracked him."

That was the revealing lightning flash. Mary Fred faltered out, "I—don't—know." But she was answering it to herself: *Not* what *sidetracked him, Dr. Nelson—who. A girl named Mary Fred Malone did. She told Ander and everybody else that the minute he finished his residency at Hart Memorial Hospital, she would be there to put the noose around his neck. And he was too decent to tell her to get lost for a few more years while he followed his dream.*

She had replaced the phone, and stood looking out the window without seeing the wind piling the tumbleweeds against the corral fence. *His wife kept on sidetracking him, Dr. Nelson. When he got the offer from Dr. Carmichael to be his assistant here in Big Basin, she was the one who whooped with joy. Because Ander's folks said that she and Ander could live on the old Erhart ranch while they spent more time in California. Mary Fred's dream was coming true, hip-hiphooray! Because she had also told Ander and everybody else that all she wanted in life was a stableful of horses and a houseful of kids. She never once asked Ander what he wanted.*

How could she have been so blind? The older doctor had turned over the night calls to Ander and the ones that meant a long drive over the plains in zero weather or searing heat. Ander went about his doctoring conscientiously. But how he had chafed when he was unable to get to Denver to see how Jodey was doing or to consult with this same Dr. Nelson about him. Ander had sat up, sometimes till dawn, poring over books and case records, relating to just such subconscious fears as Jodey's.

Yes, Ander had let clues fall all along the way, like Hansel and Gretel in the old fairy tale with their dropping of crumbs. But his wife had been too concerned about herself and her not filling up the house with children to notice. And his wife had wondered why she and Ander were so far apart, and why life had turned drab and unleavened.

She had still been staring out the window when she saw their ranch helper backing the jeep out of the shed for a trip to Big Basin. She had run out and called to him that she wanted to ride into town with him. "I'll come home with Ander," she said as she climbed in beside him.

But she hadn't found Ander in the one-story office building. The gray-haired Dr. Carmichael told her he had gone out of town on an emergency call. "Boy fell off a barn and broke his leg, and no one to bring him in. You wait over at the drugstore, because he'll be stopping there to sign prescriptions."

He added, "I guess Ander knows his old-timer will be waiting in outpatient for him to take the stitches out of his barbed-wire cut. The old fellow won't have anything to do with me because he claims I put pomade on my hair."

"He's the one who was born in a covered wagon as they crossed the plains, isn't he?"

The doctor nodded. "And thinks any man is a sissy if he can't put his boot heel on a rattlesnake's head and pull off the rattlers."

So Mary Fred was sitting at the fountain, straightening the toothpaste ad, and impatiently watching the road for Ander. She pushed back her Coke glass, emptied the silver out of her purse, and counted it. She went to the phone booth, and asked their local operator what it cost to talk to Dallas. She was given the rate and also the friendly suggestion, "It's about five now. If you wait till six, you can get the night rate."

"I can't wait till then."

Her call to Dallas was answered by her brother's wife, Miggs. They talked, with Mary Fred dropping in more quarters and dimes as their time ran out. And then she was too full of excited plans to wait in the store. She stood outside, her eyes squinting against the lowering sun, and her hair blowing every whichway in the wind. A car braked suddenly, and a voice called out, "You looking for somebody?"

"Ander! Yes, I'm looking for somebody I couldn't wait for to come home. So I hooked a ride in so I could drive back with you."

She waited in the car out of the wind while he

signed his prescriptions. He came out and tossed two candy bars in her lap. "I'll give you one for peeling mine."

She said over the rattle of their wrappings as he drove the short distance to the hospital, "How would a doctor like you, with a couple of years of medical practice, go about getting to be a child psychiatrist?"

He reached for his candy bar, and said with the indifference of one answering a hypothetical question, "Out in this neck of the woods he'd go to Colorado U for classes and lectures, and then he'd work in the Child Guidance Clinic with the patients that come in and with the ones in hospitals. In the pediatric area, of course."

"How long would it take him?"

He swallowed a bite of candy. "Three years, give or take a little."

They had reached the hospital. She got out with him, and they walked toward the steps, their heads bent low against the wind. She waited till they reached the sheltered doorway to ask further, "How long would it take *you* to settle things up here and get started? Would it be hard for Dr. Carmichael to replace you?"

He pushed the blown hair back from her face so that his amazed eyes could look into hers. "What are you talking about, idiot girl?"

"You haven't answered my question."

He stood with his hand on the door. "It wouldn't take me long. And no, it wouldn't be hard for Carmichael to find a replacement. There are always beginning doctors glad to team up with an older man like him for experience. A lot, too, that would jump at the chance of getting in a town like Big Basin where they have hunting and fishing and skiing."

Absently he pushed open the door, and they went in. The nurse at the desk said, "Old Mr. Benjamin is waiting for you in outpatient, Dr. Erhart. Every ten minutes he comes up to see if you're here yet, and each time the air gets bluer."

Ander said, "Better wait upstairs, Mary Fred. It'll be the same routine of God losing the pattern to making men and women with guts and backbone."

"In '85 He lost it," the nurse said. "That was the year our Mr. Benjamin was born."

But Mary Fred walked on down the steps with Ander. She said, "I've been planning all afternoon on us moving to Denver, and your taking the courses you'll need and doing whatever else you'll need to make yourself into what you'd be if you hadn't married me."

He said with even more amazement, "Are you off your rocker? You've heard of how it takes money to buy groceries and pay rent? And support our stableful of horses? Paying board for them in Denver would bankrupt a rich man. I could get a government grant to take care of tuition, but books alone— You hand out twenty-five bucks for one, thirty-two fifty for another—"

"You've heard of big, husky gals getting a job to help their husbands through school? And besides—"

A tall wraith of an old man in boots, Levis, and

plaid shirt bellowed at them, "I just about wore out the seat of my pants waiting for you."

He was sitting on a high stool close to the door in the outpatient room with its tiled floor and walls, its tables for minor surgery, and its antiseptic-laden air untouched by the roistering wind outside. Only a young assistant was there, and he said, "I took off his bandages, Doctor, and I laid out your instruments. There's a barbecue down the road a ways—"

Ander lifted his hand dismissingly. "Go right along. Mary Fred can hold the patient down if he needs holding."

All the while Ander scrubbed up and got into his white jacket, the deaf old man excoriated the present generation for its softness, its craving for security. When he had partially run down, Mary Fred finished her sentence, "—besides, you don't have to worry about high rents in Denver or paying board for the horses."

The old patient said, "I'd have ripped them stitches out myself if I coulda reached back of my shoulder." He didn't need holding down. He sat as straight as one of the fence posts that carried the barbed wire he had crashed into one dark night. He never flinched while Ander painstakingly snipped and lifted out stiff threads of catgut.

Ander looked over at Mary Fred who had also found herself a high white stool. "What do you mean —not worry about paying rent in Denver or board for the horses? You aren't thinking of staying on at the ranch while I'm in Denver, are you?"

"Are *you* off your rocker? I'm the whither thou goest I go along *with*. I mean I've already phoned Miggs in Dallas. She said she and Johnny would be glad to have us live on the farm while they're gone. Shandy and Miss Goldie and Sir Echo—it's home for them anyway. Oh, Ander, you should have told me that you had other longings besides being a G.P. You should have got me off your neck and gone on."

"I like you on my neck and around it." Old Mr. Benjamin was now reviling barbed wire and homesteaders. Ander nodded in agreement, and talked under it to Mary Fred, "If we stayed on here, I'd make good money. We could have new cars, more palominos, a trip to Europe every five years or so—like Carmichael. It'd be a good life. I'm not low-rating it, but it's almost too easy. Pediatric psych. is still in the pioneering stage. It's tough going, because these poor kids don't stretch out on a couch and tell everything they remember from the time they sucked their thumbs. As Nelson says, you have black depressions over your failures. And then again you hit the clouds when you see a little fellow like Jodey pushing out of his shell."

The old gentleman was now telling about his mother who left the safety and comforts of a home in Ohio to cross the plains in a covered wagon. "You don't find women like that nowadays," he grumbled.

Again his deafness and brief silence gave Mary Fred a chance to say more. "Me, and my big blabmouth. Me, and my bleating that all I wanted was a stableful of horses and a houseful of kids. Maybe what I want and what God wants for me are two different things. I've been—talking things over—with Him, too—" Her voice wavered.

There was a stronger smell of antiseptic as Ander swabbed the healing and dark zigzag cut. He flicked a tender smile toward Mary Fred. "So we go for broke. I can't think of anyone I'd rather be poor with." He bent to yell into his patient's ear, "There you are, Mr. Benjamin, good as new again."

The old-timer stood up shakily on his runover cowboy boots. Mary Fred was so brimful of happiness that she stood on tiptoe and kissed him on a leathery cheek and shouted, "Be more careful of barbed-wire fences, Pops."

A delighted and impish smile lit up his weathered face. He caught her arm with a strength she didn't think him capable of, pulled her closer, and gave her a resounding smack on her cheek in return. "Who wants to be careful, little honeybee? That's not for young folks like us."

❧ 24 ❧

Carlton went to an early Mass that next morning so
that he could devote unbroken hours to working in the
yard. When Beany with Mister and Mary Liz returned from a later one, he stilled the power mower
and walked over to the car to greet them. The wind
was only a frisky breeze this noontime. Beany spilled
out her exasperation, as she had so often before,
"That's the last time I'm taking little Miss Fidget to
church until she's grown."

Her father swung Mary Liz onto his shoulder. Her
yellow dress, with the butterfly pockets, looked as
though it had wiped up a floor—as indeed it had.
"What'd she do this time? Help herself to a dime
when the collection basket went by?"

Mister answered, "She crawled under seats." He
looked across the street to the home of the new pups.
"Today is the day each body can sit on the ground and
hold a pup."

Carlton took them both across the street, and left
them to savor their momentous occasion. He told

Beany when he returned, "We've lost two of our supper guests—Mary Fred and Ander. She called while you were gone. I had quite a time making sense out of what she was saying. But I'll translate for you. She owes Jodey a great debt."

"She does?"

"And she and Ander will be our poor relations, she says."

"Our poor relations?"

"Yes. Ander is giving up his practice to start the long haul of being a child psychiatrist. Just as soon as the doctor in Big Basin can find a replacement. They're to stay at the farm while Miggs and Johnny are gone."

"On the farm!" Beany shook her head dubiously. "Mary Fred will never be able to handle that old combination range out there. They'll be our undernourished relations. Did you talk to Ander?"

"Briefly. He asked about Jodey. I told him he had been with McNally the last couple of days. He asked again if he had laughed yet. I told him that when he did, we'd send him a wire."

Carlton went back across the street for the children. Beany was trying to poke some of the rose tendrils, loosened by the wind, back into place on the trellis when Joe Collins parked his convertible at the curb and came across the lawn to her.

Her uneasiness returned. If he asked her advice about rooming with Betty Lou and Dick, would it only worsen things if she told him she wouldn't trust the roomer they now had as far as she, Beany, could throw an elephant?

230

With this *idée fixe* in her mind, she listened uncomprehendingly while Joe told about talking with Alice Henderson at the Buckeye yesterday when he stopped for coffee. And how she had asked him if he knew how to weatherproof a screened porch, and he had said he sure did, because he had done his mother's in Peachtree.

"And then Alice asked me if I'd like to move to McNally's house and work out my room rent by fixing up the porch as I got time."

Beany knew such weak relief that she almost leaned against the trellis with its prickly covering. "That sounds like a swell idea, Joe. And you could keep Jodey with you at night and weekends."

He scowled at his cigarette before he lit it. "Yes, but what I'm afraid of is that this is something Alice Henderson cooked up. What I mean is that McNally's already done so much for Jodey." He flicked his sheepish, boyish smile at Beany. "Not to mention bringing me home that night I got so polluted at the Buckeye. I don't know whether she wants me to room there, and I'm afraid she's so darn good-hearted, she might hate to come right out and tell me. So I wondered, Beany, if maybe you could—"

"Find out how she feels about your being a renter and weatherproofer?"

"Right, Beany. Find out if this is all Alice Henderson's brainstorm."

"I'll feel her out when she comes to supper with Jodey later on." Beany couldn't help voicing her relief. "I thought maybe you were planning on moving out with Betty Lou and Dick. Where Yvonne Plettner is."

"She isn't there anymore. She and Dick had a terrible row because Vonnie slapped their little girl. She's left St. Michael's, too. I suppose because Dick was sort of her boss there. I saw him last week when I went to pay on the hospital bill. Dick told me something else that at first I just couldn't believe—"

He stopped with the reluctance of a nice man to speak ill of a girl. But Beany had to know what that *something else* was. She prodded gently, "Was it about Jodey? She hated him, you know."

"That's what I can't understand," he said in a bewildered way. And then in a confiding rush, "Dick said she was about to be fired from the Peachtree hospital because of something that came to light a couple of years after it happened. It was the night Jodey was there, and another nurse told how he was crying in the children's ward and Vonnie just up and shoved him, crib and all, into a storage closet right across the hall. This nurse said Vonnie shut the door tight and left the little fellow in the dark all night long—crying—" Joe's voice broke.

He took a shaky puff of cigarette, and went on. "Dick said he didn't believe it when he heard it, and that's why he got Yvonne her job here in Denver. But he says he believes it now. At first, I couldn't believe it either. But, Beany, somehow it all adds up."

Yes, it all added up. Jodey's terror of the dark, of hospitals, of anyone in white. And to think that a girl, bitter and hate-filled because her high-school steady had jilted her for a prettier, softer-spoken girl, had done that to him. Now it had cost her her room at Dick's and Betty Lou's, her job at St. Michael's, and her last hope of getting Joe Collins. For she must realize that Dick would tell him what he knew about her. *I could feel sorry for you, Yvonne, and your unrequited love if you hadn't taken it out on Jodey.*

Beany mused aloud, "McNally's the one who's helped Jodey the most."

"Don't I know! And that's why I don't want to embarrass her by springing this moving-in and carpentering deal on her. Of course, I wouldn't be chintzy enough to figure my work would pay for my room rent. I'd help her any way I could and not expect a dime for it." He said hesitantly, "She's had it tough. Alice told me about her being in debt up to her eyebrows—which makes two of us." And still more hesitantly, "I don't know how to say it, Beany, but McNally knows, and I know, there could never be anything but friendship. I mean, from what Alice mentioned, McNally's pretty frosted on men, and I— Well, no one could ever take Cooky's place."

"I know, Joe."

Carlton was coming across the street. He said as he shook hands with Joe, "I got to sit on the ground and hold a pup, too. The kids are watching them have their midday meal now."

The man talk turned then to the sputtery power mower. Joe went with Carlton, as he pushed it to the back yard, to try his knack at desputtering it. Beany lingered on in front, watching for the children to appear.

A day of surprises. Here came McNally's old

humped-up green car. She parked it behind the Collins' convertible. Before it came to a full stop, Jodey was out of it. A book bag was strapped over his shoulder, and he tumbled out an incoherent recital about his going to school where apples were on the ground and a donkey was careful not to step on kittens. "And McNally bought me crayons for when I sit at a desk that has a little round ditch to put a pencil in. I want to show Dad." He was running around the house as fast as he had ever run toward the spirea bushes.

McNally stood, leaning against the car. She was wearing a red slipover, and in spite of her still being thin and slower to smile, she seemed somehow more like the old McNally. Her protective coating was gone.

The two old schoolmates simply looked at each other, understanding much without putting it into words. Beany said only, "So he wasn't afraid down there?" and McNally answered on a ragged laugh, "I was the one that was afraid—until I dropped something in the wishing well."

"Come on out to the patio where you can rest your bum ankle. Joe is out in back with Carl."

"Wait. There's something I want to talk about first. That Alice and her managing my life!" For the second time Beany heard about Alice's asking Joe to move into the back bedroom upstairs while he weatherproofed the adjoining porch.

For the second time Beany said, "That sounds like a swell idea."

"It would be to me, too, on account of Jodey, if I could be sure Alice wasn't pressuring the poor fellow and that he doesn't feel obligated to me because of my doing for Jodey. Alice said he didn't give her a yes or no. I imagine the poor fellow couldn't think fast enough to get himself off the hook."

For the second time Beany laughed in wondrous relief. "Joe is afraid Alice is doing this on her own and that *you* might not be in favor of it. *He* wants to come. So what is there to worry about?"

McNally said slowly, "Just one thing, Alice. I'll have to get it through her scheming head that this is all for the mutual benefit of Joe, Jodey—and me. And that she's never even to think anything else. Joe and I both have debts to pay and scars to heal."

"I know," Beany said again. Mister and Mary Liz were calling from the opposite curb, and she said, "Let me get them. We don't dare give them permission to cross the street alone even if there isn't a car in sight."

So much enthusiasm on the Buell patio while a left-over gust of yesterday's wind flapped the awning. The small Buells had to tell of their holding roly-poly pups on their laps. The wet front of Mary Liz's rumpled dress gave evidence that she had held one overlong. Joe Collins was telling McNally how he had made a lean-to off his mother's kitchen into a room.

Jodey, usually the shrinking one, kept right on talking about the garden he had visited yesterday. "And I dropped a flower in the wishing well."

Beany asked, "Did you make a wish?"

"Oh, yes. I wished that the monkey would drop a nut down on my head like he did once on Miss McNally's."

Carlton and Joe guffawed. Mary Liz jumped up and

down in shared delight. And then a wondrous thing happened. Jodey laughed. The men's laughter stopped short in surprise. Beany's and McNally's eyes filled with tears. The miracle had come at last. *Jodey laughed.* The four grown-ups exchanged looks of wonder that drew them in close communion—as though each had taken a sip of a loving cup passed around.

The afternoon sun was still high in the sky, and the Buells were alone in the patio with the smell of newly cut grass, and only enough breeze to riffle the awning.

Joe Collins had tendered his regrets for their wiener roast later in the evening. He was anxious to take the measurements of the porch on Hawthorne, so that he could figure how much material he would need. McNally said that she, too, had much getting ready to do for this shift in her days from the Buckeye Bar and Grill to the M. Godwin Kindergarten.

Beany's packing of the mesh bag with Jodey's clothes was slowed by her wiping away tears and blowing her nose. McNally scolded her. "Beany, for heaven's sake, you'll be seeing all too much of Jodey and me, too. Every time he makes something, he'll want to bring it to you."

The Buells escorted them out to the two cars. Jodey climbed into the convertible with his father. Joe Collins said, "You go ahead, McNally, and lead the way."

Standing beside Carlton, Beany watched them disappear down Laurel Lane. . . . Joe had said, "No one could ever take Cooky's place." He was right— no one ever could—but that still didn't mean that

236

Jodey need go motherless through life. McNally had said, "Joe and I both have debts to pay and scars to heal." But debts could be paid and scars could heal after a time. . . .

She was careful not to mention such a thought to Carlton, who would reprove her for jumping to conclusions with no basis of fact. So she said instead as they reached the patio, "Fine thing! We ask four people—five, counting Jodey—for supper guests. And everyone comes up with regrets. They do not choose to eat in our back yard."

"You know something, Beany. I do not choose to eat supper in our back yard, either. I'm tired of dodging clotheslines and tripping over the sandbox. What's to hinder us from loading up and heading for the hills?"

"Why, not a thing—not a blessed thing. Hurray, hurroo! Let's get out the diamond brooch."

There was the old familiar rattle and clink as Carlton set the picnic kit onto the sink's drainboard. To their ears, it was music. He wiped off the dust. Beany started reaching for supplies in the refrigerator.

"There's no reason why we have to come back tonight," Carlton said. "No reason why we can't stay over and come back tomorrow. How'd you like to go on another honeymoon, Miss Beany?"

"You mean go up to Uncle Matthew's cabin above Cherry Springs? You mean a honeymoon for four?"

"There's no law that says a honeymoon has to be for two, is there?" He turned to the small and interested listeners. "How'd you like to go on a honeymoon with us?"

"What is a honeymoon?" Mister wanted to know.
Beany answered, "It's a trip you go on with the
one you love most—"

"Or ones," his father amended. "We'll drive up to
Uncle Matthew's cabin in the mountains, and chop
wood and cook supper on a stove that smokes, and you
kids will sleep in a bed with slats that drop out every-
time you move, and you'll get up in the morning looking like corkscrews."

"And it'll be fun, fun, fun," Beany sang out. "So,
you little peoples, start gathering up sweaters and
warm nighties."

A scampering half hour of getting ready. Carlton
phoned Uncle Matthew to ask about the cabin. Yes,
indeed, he'd be glad for them to use it. He'd watch for
them and would bring the key out to the curb so they
wouldn't be delayed by coming in. Beany took time to
send a telegram to Dr. Ander Erhart in Big Basin. It
said only, "Jodey laughed today."

Even though Carlton packed the back of the car so
the children could stretch out and sleep, they both
wanted to sit in front. "I guess on a honeymoon for
four," he conceded, "everyone should sit together."
Mary Liz sat between her parents, and Mister next to
Beany and the window. Thumper was the lone passenger in back.

Uncle Matthew was waiting in front of his high-rise
apartment house. Aunt Ruth always excused her frequent trips with, "But Matthew won't want for a
thing. He can order his meals sent up. The manage-

ment takes care of laundry and dry cleaning. There's even a barbershop there in the building." And Carlton had said to Beany, "He won't want for a thing but companionship and a little concern."

The cabin key was passed from Uncle Matthew's hand to Mister's outstretched one. Beany said as they drove on, "I thought Aunt Ruth was coming back from Mexico, Carl."

"She was. But she decided to wait until after the Labor Day jam on the airlines. If she doesn't find another excuse, she'll be home next week."

Beany glanced back at the tall figure, still standing at the curb looking after them. He looked somehow lonely and uncared for, and Beany spoke her thoughts aloud, "The next time I begrudge the poor old fellow coming in for coffee or Scotch, I hope somebody knocks my teeth out."

Carlton gave her a slanted look without taking his eyes off the road. *"Somebody* has often wanted to." But he added, "Can't you take Mary Liz on your lap?" which meant, as Beany knew, "Can't you sit closer?" She did both.

He nodded toward a filling station they passed. "Remember? That's where we stopped so I could cut the tin cans off the car and wipe off some of the Just Married signs. The lipstick they must have used on them!"

"And I shook the rice out of my hair and bra and shoes."

The restive Thumper quieted as the miles clocked

off. They passed through Cherry Springs and started the gradual and winding climb to a cabin made of pine slabs and almost hidden by trees.

Beany's thoughts were still back with the bride in her white dress and her lap full of filmy veil. She had thought then that nobody could be as happy as she was that day. She had even thought that marriage and "they lived happily ever after" went hand in hand. She hadn't known that, with its births and deaths and leave-takings and mistakes and regrets, it was an up-and-down road.

But this surprising thought came to her: I'm happier today than I was on my wedding day. That had been a giddy ecstasy; today was a sober contentment. Didn't some poet say once that no heart could know joy until it has first known sorrow?

Mister, sitting beside her, was fighting off sleep. He said in a faraway voice, "When does the honeymoon start?"

She drew him under the shelter of her coat, for the air by now had a chill undertone. "It started four years ago, honey."

Again Carlton gave her a slanted smile, and risked taking one hand off the wheel for a half minute to hug her even closer. "And, in spite of storms, doldrums, fireworks, and cold wars, it's gone on, Mister."

About the Author

Lenora Mattingly Weber was born in Dawn, Missouri. When she was twelve, her adventurous family set out to homestead on the plains of Colorado. Here, she raised motherless lambs on baby bottles, gentled broncos, and chopped railroad ties into firewood. At the age of sixteen she rode in rodeos and Wild West shows. Her well-loved stories for girls reflect her experiences with her own family. As the mother of six children and as a grandmother, she was well qualified to write of family life. Her love of the outdoors, her interest in community affairs, and her deep understanding of family relationships helped to make her characters as credible as they are memorable.

Mrs. Weber enjoyed horseback riding and swimming. She loved to cook, but her first love was writing.